Elizabeth made her way toward Jessica. "What have you done to Nora now?" she demanded.

"What are you blaming me for?" Jessica asked.

"She's just a crazy witch," Lila explained to everyone. "Everybody knows the Mercandys are weird. Let her go to the haunted house, where she belongs."

Elizabeth hesitated for a moment. She didn't believe there was any truth to the rumors about the Mercandys, and now she had to help out her friend. She turned on her heel and ran out the front door after Nora.

Jessica started after her sister.

"Let her go," Lila said. "Let's get back to the party."

But who knew what could happen to Elizabeth if she went near the Mercandy mansion on Halloween night!

SWEET VALLEY TWINS

The Haunted House

Written by
Jamie Suzanne

Created by
FRANCINE PASCAL

A BANTAM SKYLARK BOOK®
TORONTO · NEW YORK · LONDON · SYDNEY · AUCKLAND

RL 4, 008–012

THE HAUNTED HOUSE
A Bantam Skylark Book / October 1986

Skylark Books is a registered trademark of Bantam Books, Inc. Registered in U.S. Patent and Trademark Office and elsewhere.

Sweet Valley High and Sweet Valley Twins are trademarks of Francine Pascal

Conceived by Francine Pascal

Produced by Cloverdale Press Inc.

Cover art by James Mathewuse

ISBN 0-553-15446-X

Published simultaneously in the United States and Canada

Bantam Books are published by Bantam Books, Inc. Its trade-mark, consisting of the words "Bantam Books" and the por-trayal of a rooster, is Registered in U.S. Patent and Trademark Office and in other countries. Marca Registrada. Bantam Books, Inc., 666 Fifth Avenue, New York, New York 10103.

PRINTED IN THE UNITED STATES OF AMERICA

O   0 9 8 7 6 5 4 3 2

One

◇

It was nearly four-thirty when the Wakefield twins left the library. "We'd better hurry," declared Elizabeth. "We told Mom we'd be home by four o'clock."

"Don't worry," said Jessica. "When Mom reads our reports, she'll know we really used the extra time working. This report will definitely get us an A in social studies."

"Do you really think 'the Hairnet' will give us an A?" Elizabeth asked. Mrs. Arnette, their social studies teacher, always wore a hairnet over her gray hair. Long ago one of her students started calling Mrs. Arnette the Hairnet behind her back. The nickname had stuck and both girls giggled whenever they heard it.

Jessica and Elizabeth rode their bicycles along

the shady tree-lined streets of their pretty California town. The Wakefield twins were well known in Sweet Valley, and few people could tell them apart. They were absolutely identical, with long blond hair, blue-green eyes, and dimples in their left cheeks.

Since they had become sixth graders at Sweet Valley Middle School, Jessica had started to wear her hair in loose curls. She had also started to wear lip gloss and the tiniest brush of mascara.

Elizabeth, on the other hand, was not so fond of wearing makeup. She was content with her natural peaches-and-cream complexion, and she didn't feel she needed to highlight her already long lashes. She wore her hair pulled back to each side and fastened with barrettes.

In the past few months each twin had begun to realize that while they looked identical, they were two separate people with two very different personalities. Elizabeth tended to be more thoughtful than her twin. She loved to read and write and have long conversations with her friends. Jessica, on the other hand, tended to be very excitable and wasn't happy unless she was *doing* something. She always had a dozen things planned, and as soon as one was finished, she rushed on to the next. She loved to talk about boys and clothes and hang out with her friends in the Unicorn Club. Elizabeth thought that the girls Jessica liked were awfully silly, and Jessica thought that Elizabeth's friends were awfully boring, but despite their differences the twins were best friends.

As they turned their bicycles onto Camden Drive, Jessica and Elizabeth slowed down. Usually the twins avoided Camden Drive altogether because the Mercandy mansion was located there. The Mercandy mansion was old and rundown. It looked like an old haunted house in the movies. Jessica and Elizabeth had heard lots of rumors about the people that lived there. Most of them involved Mrs. Mercandy. She was said to be a witch who kept her crazy husband locked in the attic. The strange lights and shadows that appeared in the attic windows on some nights seemed to prove the stories true.

All the rumors about the Mercandys and their house frightened the girls, but they were still curious about the place and the people living there. And even though they deliberately stayed across the street and kept as much distance between themselves and the mansion as possible, today they were especially curious.

Less than a week ago Jessica and Elizabeth had seen a taxi drive down the street and stop in front of the forbidding house. The twins had watched a dark-haired girl about their own age get out of the cab and walk to the dilapidated front porch. The cab driver had deposited a cardboard suitcase on the curb and driven off in a hurry.

When the twins had looked back toward the porch, the dark-haired girl disappeared into the dimly lit house.

The twins had talked about this incident every day since it had happened. They hadn't seen the girl again, and they were beginning to wonder if old lady Mercandy had done something dreadful to her.

Many years ago the mansion had been a beautiful Spanish-tiled home located on a wooded acre of well-manicured trees and gardens. Now the white stucco house was grayed and crumbling with age. Red roof tiles were missing, and the front porch looked ready to collapse at any moment. The grounds, mostly hidden behind an iron fence, were overrun with untended shrubbery, bushes, and tall weeds.

As they coasted along on their bikes, Elizabeth and Jessica kept their heads turned toward the mansion. They strained to see beyond the fence and thick green foliage.

Suddenly Jessica gasped. "Lizzie, look!" she cried.

Both pairs of blue-green eyes focused on the entrance to the mansion. The heavy oak door had opened, and the same dark-haired girl they had seen earlier stepped out onto the porch. Her hair was pulled back in a ponytail that ended below her waist. She was wearing a pair of worn jeans and a faded plaid blouse.

The girl was unaware that she was being watched. She seemed to be looking for something in the front yard. She stepped lightly down the porch steps and called out something that neither Elizabeth nor Jessica could hear.

Without realizing it the twins had come to a complete standstill in the middle of the street. Finally Elizabeth said, "Jess, we can't just stop here and stare."

"I know," Jessica agreed. She carefully got off her bicycle and stepped onto the sidewalk. She bent down on one knee and untied her tennis shoe. "Oops, I have to tie my shoelace." She flashed a smile up at her twin. "Somehow it got untied." As she fooled around with her shoelace, Jessica heard the girl call out a second time.

"I think she's calling her dog," Jessica said. "It sounded like she said, 'Here, Boris.'"

"Boris?" Elizabeth said in a whisper. "Who would name a dog Boris?"

"The Mercandy witch, that's who," Jessica replied quickly.

"Well, I think it's a creepy name," Elizabeth replied.

"Of course it is," Jessica said matter-of-factly. "It's a creepy name and a creepy place, and everybody who lives there is creepy." She was still down on one knee. "I can't keep tying my shoe all day. . . . I'm beginning to feel like an idiot."

"I've got an idea," said Elizabeth. She

dropped a stack of books all over the sidewalk. "Oh, no," she cried, biting her lip to keep from giggling. As she and Jessica gathered the scattered books and papers, the dark-haired girl came back into view. She was carrying a black cat in her arms. As she started back up the steps, the front door opened.

"Do you see the witch inside?" Jessica asked, holding her breath.

The twins peered at the dark silhouette standing in the partially opened doorway. "I don't know . . ." Elizabeth replied hesitantly. "It does look like an old woman. And she's dressed all in black."

"I hope she doesn't see us!" Jessica clutched at her sister as the door closed on the dark-haired girl and the woman dressed in black. The old house seemed to have swallowed them up. The twins stared at each other, their eyes huge. At last Elizabeth said, "Let's go home and see what Steven knows about the Mercandys."

The twins' fourteen-year-old brother, Steven, didn't arrive home until an hour later. Elizabeth and Jessica nearly attacked him as he opened the front door.

"Steven, guess what?" Elizabeth was flushed with excitement.

Steven did not get excited very easily. He tossed a basketball and his jacket into the hall closet before he finally asked, "What?"

"A few days ago Jessica and I saw a girl arrive at the Mercandy mansion with a suitcase. We saw her again today on our way home from the library. She's just about our age," Elizabeth added.

Jessica took over. "She has this long black hair that goes all the way down to her waist. We think that old Mrs. Mercandy has cast a spell on her or something."

"We do?" asked Elizabeth.

"Of course," Jessica declared. "Why else would anybody stay in that creepy house with the Mercandy witch?"

Mr. Wakefield came into the kitchen just in time to hear Jessica's last words. "What's this about a witch?"

"The girls have talked about nothing else since they got home," said Mrs. Wakefield. She was in the kitchen, preparing dinner.

Elizabeth and Jessica quickly told their father about the new girl at the Mercandy mansion.

After the girls finished detailing the events of that afternoon, Mr. Wakefield said, "Why would you think Mrs. Mercandy is a witch?"

"Daddy," Jessica explained, as though her father were six, "everybody knows that the Mercandy mansion is haunted and that old Mrs. Mercandy is a witch."

Mr. Wakefield looked up at his wife. "Did you know we have a witch living right here in Sweet Valley?" he asked with a smile.

Mrs. Wakefield's eyes sparkled. "There certainly are lots of rumors about the Mercandys."

"They're more than rumors, Mom," Steven informed her. "The Howells live next door to the Mercandy place. Joe told me that he sees strange shadows in their attic at least once a week."

"And Janet says that she hasn't seen Mr. or Mrs. Mercandy leave the house in five whole years!" Jessica interrupted.

"And Joe's seen old lady Mercandy only once," said Steven. "One day, about two years ago, she was walking around in the backyard. And listen to this. She was as white as a ghost and her eyes were pink!"

"Steven," Mrs. Wakefield said, "please don't refer to her as old lady Mercandy."

"That's what everyone calls her, Mom," Steven protested.

"I don't care," Mrs. Wakefield said firmly. "I'd like you to show more respect for someone that age."

"I read once that witches have pale eyes that glow in the dark," said Elizabeth. "It's hard for them to see in sunlight, and that's why they come out only at night."

Mr. Wakefield groaned. "I don't want you kids to believe everything you see or hear or read. I hope all of you will use your own good intelligence before jumping to conclusions like the ones I've just heard. Now you'll have to excuse us. Your mother and I have to meet some friends for dinner."

After dinner Elizabeth changed clothes and went down to the basement to practice for the ballet class she and Jessica took twice a week. Steven went to his room to study, and Jessica headed for her favorite spot in the house, the hallway telephone.

It was late October and the sun was sinking out of sight as Jessica snapped on the table lamp and picked up the telephone receiver. She dialed Lila Fowler's number.

Jessica and Lila had known each other in elementary school, but had become good friends only since Jessica joined the Unicorn Club. As far as Jessica was concerned, the Unicorn Club was the best thing that had ever happened to her. The members were the most popular girls in school. They were usually the center of attention. Because most of them were seventh and eighth graders, Jessica got to go to a lot of places where sixth graders weren't usually welcome.

Lila picked up the phone on the third ring. "Lila!" Jessica exclaimed. "Guess what? Today Elizabeth and I saw that same girl outside the Mercandy mansion."

"Really?"

Jessica could tell that Lila was as excited as she was about this new development.

"What did you find out about her?"

"We saw her in the front yard. She picked up a black cat named Boris. Then an old woman called her inside. She was all dressed in black."

"The Mercandy witch! What did she look like?"

"I couldn't tell," Jessica admitted. "It was awfully dark."

"Did you say anything to the girl?" Lila asked.

"No," said Jessica. "Before we got a chance the Mercandy witch snatched her up." Jessica knew she was exaggerating, but she also knew her story would make Lila incredibly jealous.

"Wow!" exclaimed Lila. "Do you think she's a witch too?"

"Maybe," said Jessica. "Come to think of it, she looked awfully spooky!"

"I wonder if Janet knows about this," Lila said abruptly. "Have you talked to her yet?"

"No, I was going to call her next," Jessica replied.

"Well, don't bother," Lila ordered. "*I'll* call her. After all, she is my cousin. She lives right next door to the Mercandy mansion. By now I bet she's seen this girl too. I'll see you in school tomorrow."

When Jessica hung up, she was annoyed that Lila was going to talk to Janet before she could, but Jessica didn't like making Lila mad. Janet Howell was Lila's first cousin and the president of the Unicorn Club. She was the most important girl in

Sweet Valley Middle School. Jessica would never risk getting on Janet's bad side either.

Half an hour later Elizabeth was curled up on the living room couch with a book, when she caught sight of her sister in her bathing suit. Her eyebrows rose in alarm. "You're not going swimming, are you?"

"Yes, I am," Jessica replied. She headed for the sliding glass door and snapped on the backyard lights.

"Mom and Dad will have a fit. You know the pool heater was turned off this week. The water will be cold. . . you'll catch pneumonia!"

"Elizabeth," Jessica said with exaggerated patience, "this is California, not Alaska. You're supposed to be able to swim year-round. Besides, I like cold water. I'm only going to swim ten laps, and then I'll get right out."

"Did you ask Steven if it was OK?"

Jessica gave her twin a look of annoyance. "Of course I didn't. You know what he'd say."

"Well, I just don't want to get into trouble when Mom and Dad find out."

Jessica called over her shoulder as she went out onto the patio. "Don't tell them, and they'll never know."

Elizabeth watched her twin make a perfect swan dive into their aboveground pool. She glanced at the clock. It was nine-thirty. Her parents might be home anytime and the twins had promised they'd be in bed by ten o'clock. Elizabeth seldom got into trouble, and when she did, it was almost always connected with one of her sister's schemes. She breathed a sigh of relief when Jessica did her last lap and came back inside. The twins went upstairs, poked their heads into Steven's room to say good night, and then went to their separate bedrooms.

As promised, Jessica was in bed by ten, but she was wearing her Walkman headphones, with the volume turned up high. Halfway through a Johnny Buck tape she fell asleep.

Sometime later Jessica awoke with a start. Her room was pitch black. She lifted herself on her elbow and turned over to see what had awakened her. She found herself staring into two glowing red eyeballs. A hoarse voice whispered, "I am the witch of the Mercandy mansion!"

Two

◇

At the sound of Jessica's scream, Elizabeth leaped from her bed and dashed through the bathroom that separated their two rooms. When she saw a greenish face with a hideous grin and two glowing red eyes standing over Jessica, she gasped in terror. Without thinking she reached out and snapped on the bedroom light.

"Steven!" Elizabeth cried, half in surprise, half in relief.

Steven dropped the grotesque mask on the floor and fell on top of Jessica's bed, doubled over with laughter.

When Jessica recovered, she screamed angrily, "That was really mean, Steven!" She grabbed a pillow and started to pound her brother over the head with it. "I could have had a heart attack!"

Elizabeth picked up the mask her brother had been wearing and inspected it closely. "That's the scariest mask I've ever seen. Where did you get it?"

"I've been working on it all night," Steven answered proudly. "It's for my Creature from the Black Lagoon costume. I'm going to wear it to Jake Hill's Halloween party."

Jessica sat up in bed. "Elizabeth and I are going to Lila Fowler's Halloween party. So far she's invited over forty kids."

Steven took his mask from Elizabeth. In his best big-brother voice he said, "You guys better get back to bed now. Mom and Dad will be getting home soon."

Jessica made a face at him, then she turned to her sister.

"Lizzie, would you mind spending the night in here?" It was obvious that she wasn't over her fright.

With the Creature from the Black Lagoon still fresh in her mind, Elizabeth, too, was just as happy not to have to spend the night alone. "I wouldn't mind at all." She grinned at Jessica and hopped into bed next to her.

The next morning Jessica awoke with a moan. "My throat hurts," she said in a hoarse voice.

"Would you ask Mom to come up and take my temperature?"

Elizabeth gave her twin an I-told-you-so look, but kept quiet about Jessica's late night swim. She did, however, duck into the bathroom for Jessica's wet swimsuit and hang it in her twin's closet where Mrs. Wakefield wouldn't find it.

When Mrs. Wakefield came upstairs and decided that Jessica should stay home for the day, Jessica collapsed on her pillow with a sigh. She said in a hoarse voice, "Now I won't get to meet with the Unicorns. We were going to have a special meeting at lunchtime today."

"I guess you just got lucky, Jess," Elizabeth teased.

Jessica frowned at her sister. "Why can't you at least try to like the Unicorns?"

"I told you before, I think the club is pointless and silly. All you do at your meetings is gossip."

"Well, thanks a lot," Jessica said, sounding insulted.

Elizabeth's eyes twinkled as she gave her twin a grin. "I didn't mean *you*, Jess."

Jessica had already forgotten the insult to the Unicorns. "If you pass by the mansion and see that girl again, make sure you find out everything you can about her. Oh, and talk to Lila and Janet and see if they've found out anything new, and . . ."

"OK, OK." Elizabeth's eyes sparkled. "I'll let

you know everything as soon as I get home." Elizabeth zipped a white cotton tennis jacket over her pale blue shirt. "I'll see you later, Jess."

Elizabeth didn't want to walk past the Mercandy mansion by herself, so she took the longer route to school. And she didn't get a chance before homeroom started to ask Lila or Janet anything about the girl at the Mercandy mansion. But it turned out that within ten minutes of arriving at Sweet Valley Middle School, Elizabeth found out all she needed to know.

At the start of homeroom Ms. Pauley announced that a new student was going to join the class. Five minutes later the school secretary walked in. Behind her was the girl Elizabeth and Jessica had seen at the Mercandy mansion.

While the secretary went to Ms. Pauley's desk and handed her some papers, the new girl stood awkwardly in the front of the classroom looking down at the ground. Elizabeth noticed that she was wearing the same worn outfit that she had on when she had arrived at the Mercandy mansion.

When the secretary left, Ms. Pauley stood up and placed a friendly hand on the new girl's shoulder. "Boys and girls, this is Nora Mercandy. Nora has recently moved here from Pennsylvania."

There were some murmurs of surprise at the Mercandy name.

Under her breath but loud enough for those

seated around her to hear, Lila whispered, "I think she means *Transylvania*."

The teacher glanced sternly in the direction of the muffled laughter. She waited until she had everyone's attention. "I'd like one of you to volunteer to show Nora around today and help her get acquainted with Sweet Valley."

Everyone avoided Ms. Pauley's eyes as she gazed around the room and waited for a volunteer.

As the wait lengthened, students squirmed uncomfortably in their seats. Nora Mercandy continued to stare at the floor, but her face had turned scarlet. Elizabeth, unable to bear Nora's embarrassment any longer, slowly raised her hand.

Ms. Pauley smiled in relief. "Thank you, Elizabeth." To Nora she said, "Elizabeth Wakefield will show you around today and help you meet your classmates. I'm sure you'll soon feel right at home."

Ms. Pauley pointed Nora in the direction of an empty desk in the second row. As Nora walked down the aisle, Lila Fowler, and Ellen Riteman, another member of the Unicorn Club, scooted their desks as far away from her as possible. Nora looked at them in dismay.

The bell rang a few minutes later. Elizabeth picked up her books and started to make her way across the room to where Nora was seated. She was stopped by Lila. "You're not really going to show her around, are you?" Lila asked.

Elizabeth knew that Lila could be very selfish and mean—especially toward people she didn't like. And Elizabeth could tell that Lila didn't like Nora Mercandy. But she decided to ignore Lila's comment just then. She nodded. "Ms. Pauley wants me to introduce her to some of the kids. Do you want to meet her now?"

"No, thank you," Lila said stiffly. "She might cast a spell on me."

"Aren't you afraid of the Mercandy witch?" Ellen whispered. "I can't believe you volunteered to show her around."

"I think Nora looks more like a scared girl than a witch," Elizabeth replied.

"Well, if I see a frog hopping down the hall today," said Ellen, "I'm going to make sure to put *you* in my pocket and bring you home. Jessica will probably still want you around even if you are green and slimy."

Lila and Ellen broke out into laughter. They ran over to Charlie Cashman, a boy known for being a bit of a bully. A moment later the three of them stared at Nora as they walked from the classroom chanting in low creepy voices, "Boooo, boooo, boooo."

When Elizabeth reached Nora's side, she gave her a friendly smile. "Don't pay any attention to them. Most of the kids at Sweet Valley aren't so bad once you get to know them."

Nora didn't seem reassured. She looked timidly at Elizabeth and glanced quickly away. Then she picked up her book bag and notebook, and followed Elizabeth out of the classroom.

As usual the corridor was alive with students rushing from one class to another. Elizabeth took a look at Nora's schedule. "We don't have any classes together until gym this afternoon," she said, "but I'll walk you to your first class."

Elizabeth's heart sank when she saw Lila and Charlie Cashman already seated in the front row of Nora's social studies class. She just hoped they wouldn't cause the new girl any problems.

For the next hour Elizabeth had little time to think about Nora Mercandy. She was too involved in her favorite class, English. Elizabeth's love of writing had led her to start the sixth-grade newspaper, *The Sweet Valley Sixers*, with her friends Amy Sutton and Julie Porter. Although the *Sixers* had come out only twice so far, it was a big success with the sixth graders.

A few minutes past noon Elizabeth found Nora seated all alone at a table in the far corner of the cafeteria. She sat down next to her. "Hi." Elizabeth's smile was bright. "How did everything go in social studies?"

Nora was close to tears, but she managed to raise her head proudly. Her gaze met Elizabeth's long enough for her to give a bitter reply. "Everything was terrible in social studies class . . . and in English class too. Everyone treats me as if . . . as if I have some kind of disease."

Nora toyed with the food on her tray for a moment before she went on. "See those girls over there?" Elizabeth followed her gaze until she saw Lila and Ellen Riteman with the other Unicorns three tables away. "They were passing a note around in class. I don't know what it said, but every time someone read it, they'd give me an awful look."

"Nora . . ." Elizabeth hesitated, not quite knowing what to say. "Lila and Ellen are members of the Unicorn Club. A lot of popular girls belong to it. They don't do much except gossip."

"But how can they gossip about me?" Nora asked. "They don't even know me."

"When the Unicorns don't know what to gossip about, they just make something up." Elizabeth could see that this explanation only made Nora more upset.

Nora glanced again toward the Unicorns. "Why are they wearing so much purple?"

"That's the club color. They decided purple was 'in' this year." Elizabeth's dimple deepened as she added, "That's only one of the dumb things about the Unicorns."

Suddenly a paper airplane did a nosedive right into the middle of Nora's hamburger. She and Elizabeth looked around to see who sent it, but the cafeteria was strangely quiet, and the kids around them seemed to be concentrating on their lunches.

Elizabeth noticed that the airplane was a note. She unfolded it and silently read the message written on the paper. "We know about you," it said. "Go back to Transylvania."

Before Nora could read the note, Elizabeth wadded it up and tossed it into the trash can. Then she excused herself and marched over to the Unicorns' table. "Nora's a nice girl. Why don't you come over and meet her?"

"No way," Lila was quick to reply.

"If you want to be the teacher's pet and be best friends with a witch, that's fine with me," Ellen informed Elizabeth. "But don't expect us to help you. We know too much about the Mercandys. We wouldn't be seen with one of them."

Elizabeth raised an eyebrow. "What exactly do you know about the Mercandys?"

A superior smile spread across Lila's face. "That's for us to know and for you to find out."

Elizabeth turned on her heel and went to rejoin Nora. Since they had both lost their appetites, Elizabeth suggested that they start to walk over to their gym class a little early.

"Did you bring a gym suit with you today?" Elizabeth asked as they approached the girls' locker room.

Nora shook her head. "No. The one I had at

my old school was practically in rags. I tossed it out when I packed to come out here. My grandparents don't have much money . . . and I don't like to ask them for anything."

"We're not allowed to play if we're not in gym clothes," Elizabeth explained. "Not playing can affect your grade." Her face suddenly brightened. "My sister and I have extra gym suits. I'll bring you one to wear until you can get a new one."

"Are you sure your mother or your sister won't mind?" Nora asked softly.

Elizabeth shook her head. Her long blond hair swayed from side to side. "I'll check, but I'm sure it will be fine."

Elizabeth was reluctant to ask Nora anything about her personal life, but she did want to get to know her. She took a deep breath before saying, "How come you're living with your grandparents?"

Nora swallowed hard. For a second Elizabeth was afraid Nora was going to cry. "My father died when I was a baby . . . my mother died last month."

Elizabeth was stunned. "I—I'm sorry," she stammered.

Before they could say anything else, a group of girls trooped into the locker room. During gym Nora sat on the sidelines watching the other girls play tennis. Elizabeth wanted to talk to her when the period ended, but she had to hurry to drop off an article for *The Sweet Valley Sixers*. On the way out she just told Nora, "I'll bring the gym clothes tomorrow. I'll see you in homeroom in the morning."

Things didn't go well for Nora the rest of the afternoon. In her last class of the day Lila deliberately tripped her as she walked to the back of the room. As Nora grabbed on to the corner of the closest desk to keep herself from falling, Mary Giaccio, a Unicorn, whispered nastily, "Get your hands off my desk."

Even the teacher, who was nearsighted and didn't see what had actually happened, spoke harshly to her. "Young lady, I realize you're new here, but you'll find that I don't tolerate disturbances in my classroom."

The worst moment came during the walk home from school. Lila and Ellen fell into step about twenty feet behind Nora. They were joined by Bruce Patman, a spoiled, wealthy seventh grader; Charlie Cashman; and one of their friends, Jerry McAllister. Whenever Nora walked faster to try to get away from them, her small group of tormentors increased their pace.

"I wish she'd go back to Transylvania where she belongs," Lila said in a loud voice. "We don't need any more weird Mercandys living in Sweet Valley."

As she approached Camden Drive, Nora broke into a run. She darted across the street toward her grandparents' house and dashed up the pathway. By the time she reached the front door she was trembling. The one thing Nora Mercandy had learned in school that day was how much she hated it and the whole town of Sweet Valley.

Three

Elizabeth was eager to fill Jessica in on all that had happened at school that day, but first she wanted to talk to her mother. She was glad her mother had taken the day off from work to stay home with Jessica. Elizabeth found her in the flower garden near the pool.

Mrs. Wakefield greeted her daughter warmly. "Hi, honey. How was school?"

Elizabeth replied with a frown. "It was fine for me, but Nora, the Mercandys' granddaughter, started school today and I think it was awful for her." She spent the next ten minutes describing Nora and the way Lila and her group had treated her. She also explained that her grandparents didn't have much money, and that Nora needed some gym clothes. She told her mother about her offer to lend Nora a gym suit.

Mrs. Wakefield said, "That was thoughtful of you, Elizabeth. Why don't you lay out some gym clothes right now so you won't forget them in the morning?"

"OK. Thanks, Mom." Before heading inside, Elizabeth asked, "How is Jessica feeling?"

Mrs. Wakefield sighed. "Well enough to watch *Ryan's Hope, General Hospital, One Life to Live,* and *All My Children.*"

Elizabeth giggled. Jessica's fondness for soap operas was a favorite family joke.

A few minutes later she plopped down on the foot of Jessica's bed. Before she could say a word, Jessica exclaimed, "Elizabeth, I'm so glad you're here! I was just on the phone with Caroline Pearce and she told me that the girl we saw at the Mercandy mansion showed up at school, and she really is a witch. She said she acts really weird."

Caroline Pearce lived two doors away from the Wakefields. Aside from being terribly prissy, Caroline had the biggest mouth in town.

Elizabeth sighed. "I can't believe how fast Caroline can spread rumors. The girl *was* at school. Her name is Nora Mercandy, and she's the Mercandys' granddaughter. But she doesn't act weird at all. In fact, she's very nice. If you ask me, it's Lila Fowler and Ellen who are the weird ones. They were really nasty to Nora."

"Nobody asked you," Jessica replied. "And Lila and Ellen are a lot more fun than that tomboy Amy Sutton," she snapped.

Elizabeth didn't want to start an argument with her twin, especially about her friend Amy, so she didn't reply. But she gave Jessica a look that let her sister know it would be best not to say another word about Amy Sutton.

Jessica wasn't in the mood to argue either. "Caroline said she was giving everyone an evil stare. . . as if she was about to cast a spell," Jessica said. Elizabeth rolled her eyes.

"Caroline's crazy. Nora was just nervous," Elizabeth said.

Jessica didn't look convinced. She played with a strand of golden hair that had fallen across her shoulder. "How come you showed her around today? Weren't you scared?"

"No. I told you Nora's really nice," Elizabeth replied.

"Well, if Nora Mercandy's so wonderful, why did Amy avoid both of you all day?" Jessica said.

"Is that what Caroline told you? I swear, that girl can't get a story straight." Amy Sutton was Elizabeth's closest friend. They sat near each other whenever they had the chance, always ate lunch at the same table, and worked on *The Sweet Valley Sixers* together. "Amy went on a field trip today with Mr. Jackson's class," Elizabeth explained.

Elizabeth spent the next half hour trying to

convince Jessica that Nora Mercandy was not spooky, weird, or a witch. But after their talk Elizabeth still wasn't sure that her twin would give Nora a chance, especially since Lila Fowler and the Unicorns had started in on Nora. Elizabeth loved Jessica, and was very proud of her twin. There were times, though, when Elizabeth worried that Jessica allowed herself to be influenced too much by Lila and the Unicorns.

The following morning it was Elizabeth who awoke with a sore throat. She wanted to go to school, but when Mrs. Wakefield took her temperature and found she had a fever, Elizabeth settled in for a day at home.

As Jessica was getting ready to go downstairs to breakfast, Elizabeth called her into her room. "Don't forget to take these gym clothes to Nora . . . and be nice to her."

"I'm always nice to witches!" Jessica said as she waved good-bye.

Jessica took the bag Elizabeth had given her downstairs and put it on the stairs near the front door. Twenty minutes later she dashed out the side door, completely forgetting all about Nora's gym clothes.

Jessica strolled into homeroom with Lila and Ellen. When she went to her desk, she noticed Nora Mercandy seated quietly in the back of the room. It suddenly occurred to her that she had forgotten to bring Elizabeth's package. She'd have to say something about it or Lizzie would be mad. Jessica gave Nora a long, appraising look. She thought Nora looked sad and lonely. It was probably tough for a witch to be with normal people.

Just as Nora got up the courage to give her a shy smile, Jessica turned her attention back to Lila and Ellen. Nora's heart sank. Elizabeth Wakefield, the one friend she thought she had made at Sweet Valley Middle School, had pretended she didn't even know her.

The bell rang. Ms. Pauley started the day with a discussion about next week's Halloween party. "Each homeroom," she explained, "will select winners in the following categories: the ugliest, the prettiest, the scariest, and the most original."

Lila's hand went up. "Will the winners get prizes?"

"Yes," Ms. Pauley said. "The PTA has made up some special ribbons to be given to the winner of each category."

Jessica raised her hand.

"Yes, Jessica?" Ms. Pauley nodded in her direction.

That was strange, Nora thought. The teacher had called Elizabeth by the wrong name.

"Ms. Pauley," Jessica said, "when we're dressed in our costumes, will it be all right if we don't sit in our assigned seats? That way people won't know right away who we are."

"That's a good idea," Ms. Pauley agreed.

"Will there be any food at this party?" the slightly overweight Jerry McAllister wanted to know.

"There will be plenty of treats for everyone," Ms. Pauley assured the class. "Now, as you know, all sixth-period classes have been canceled on Halloween day. Students will return to their homerooms for the party. The costume judging will take place first thing in the morning, but the actual party won't take place until sixth period."

"Ms. Pauley," Amy Sutton said, "Elizabeth and I are the only kids from homeroom on the class newspaper. I thought everyone would like to know that *The Sweet Valley Sixers* is going to take pictures and carry stories about the costume winners."

Nora took special notice when Amy spoke. She knew Elizabeth and Amy were close friends. Elizabeth had promised to introduce Nora to Amy today. She had said the three of them would get together for lunch.

When lunchtime arrived, Nora waited eagerly at an otherwise empty table, hoping Elizabeth hadn't forgotten her promise. She was surprised and disappointed when Elizabeth walked in with Lila and Ellen. They took seats together at the same table all of the Unicorns had sat at the day before. Never once did Elizabeth even bother to look in her direction. Nora couldn't understand it.

How had the friendly girl from the previous day changed so much?

It wasn't until she was in the girls' locker room that Jessica remembered to tell Nora Mercandy about the forgotten gym suit.

Nora sat alone on a bench looking miserable. Jessica was in no hurry to speak to her. She knew it would make the Unicorns angry. Besides, what if Nora really was a witch?

Finally Jessica took a deep breath and walked over to where Nora was sitting. "Hi . . . I'm Jessica Wakefield," she said, her voice wavering slightly. "My sister reminded me before I left home this morning to bring you one of our extra gym suits. I forgot it, but I promise we'll get it to you tomorrow."

Nora looked puzzled. "Your sister?"

Jessica was more relaxed now. She knew Nora wouldn't do anything strange to her. "Yes, Elizabeth and I are twins. You haven't seen us together because I was home sick yesterday. Elizabeth is home sick today."

Nora's serious brown eyes carefully studied Jessica Wakefield. She had the same beautifully tanned skin, blue-green eyes, and silky blond hair as Elizabeth. For one brief moment Nora was afraid this might be some trick that the Unicorns had dreamed up to embarrass her. But she remembered that Elizabeth had mentioned a sister. She stammered, "It's—it's so hard to believe. . . . You look exactly alike. How do people tell you apart?"

Jessica was used to this sort of question. "A lot of times they don't," she replied. "Only people who know us really well can tell us apart. We have a grandmother who still gets us mixed up."

Jessica quickly picked up a tennis racket from a nearby rack. "Sorry about the gym suit," she repeated. With a wave she headed out toward the tennis courts.

Lila and Ellen joined Jessica outside the gym. "Why were you talking to the Mercandy witch?" Ellen wanted to know.

"Elizabeth wanted me to bring her one of our extra gym suits and I left it at home," Jessica explained.

"The witch can't even afford a gym suit?" Ellen sneered.

"I bet it's a trick," Lila declared. "She probably wants your gym suit so she can work black magic on you!"

"Be serious, Lila," Jessica snapped.

"I hope you're not defending the Mercandy witch, Jessica." Lila's tone was threatening.

Jessica knew that Elizabeth liked Nora, and she seemed harmless enough. On the other hand, she didn't want to get on the Unicorns' bad side. "Come on," she said, starting to jog to the courts. "Let's play tennis."

Ms. Langberg quickly assigned each of the girls to a court. Lila, who was to have played against Elizabeth, was left without an opponent.

"Mercandy," the gym teacher called, motioning to Nora to come join her. As Nora approached, Ms. Langberg explained, "I don't usually allow students to play unless they're in their gym attire, but since we have uneven numbers here today, I'd like you to play against Lila."

"Ms. Langberg, maybe you should ask her if she's ever played before," Lila said in a superior tone.

"Thank you, Lila," the teacher said sarcastically. "I was just about to do that."

"Yes, ma'am," Nora replied quickly. "Back home I took lessons from the Parks and Recreation Department."

After the teacher left the two girls alone, Lila sniffed, "I have my own tennis court. I take lessons from a private instructor. He used to be a professional tennis player."

Nora remained silent and started for the opposite side of the net.

"Just a minute," Lila said. "Would you like to make a bet on who wins the set?"

Nora hesitated. "I—I don't have any money."

"That's okay. We can bet for something else," Lila insisted. "I have an expensive cloisonné pen. I'll bet that against the charm you're wearing."

Nora's fingers flew to the unicorn charm that hung around her neck. "No," she added quickly, "this was a gift from my mother."

"Well," Lila said scornfully, "you must have something you can bet."

Nora thought for a moment. "I have a silver-plated compact in my book bag. It has a mirror and an attached comb."

"I already have a compact," said Lila, "but I guess that will have to do." She raised her nose into the air. "My pen against your compact. Is it a deal?"

"OK," Nora agreed reluctantly.

Nora had watched Lila play the day before, and she knew Lila was good. But if there was one thing Nora Mercandy knew she could do, it was play tennis. She had won the Philadelphia Parks and Recreation Department's junior championship the previous summer.

Lila won the toss for serve. When Nora returned her first serve straight down the line, Lila realized that it might not be so easy to beat Nora Mercandy.

By the fourth game of the set, the score was three to one in favor of Nora. When the score had reached five to one, the other girls in the class gathered with the gym teacher to watch the last game. In the final play of the set Nora raced to the net and smashed an overhead that bounced off Lila's left foot and into the air, out of reach.

Everyone including Ms. Langberg started clapping. Nora grinned shyly and picked up a ball from her side of the court.

Lila's face was red with rage. She screamed, "Just wait, Mercandy witch . . . I'll get you!"

Nora's smile faded. She walked quickly away.

Twenty minutes later, after nearly everyone else had left the locker room, Lila approached Nora. She seemed to have calmed down. She even wore a smile as she handed her cloisonné pen to Nora. But something in Lila's eyes let Nora know that Lila's smile was fake, and that Lila was still fuming inside.

When she looked at the pen, Nora said, "You can keep it, Lila. It looks too good to give away."

"It doesn't matter," Lila answered with a careless shrug. "My father will just buy me another one." Still wearing the same insincere smile, she said, "Take it, Nora. A deal is a deal."

Nora hesitated before taking the expensive pen from Lila. She had no idea how much she would later regret winning the tennis bet.

Four

◇

Elizabeth and Amy waited outside homeroom hoping to see Nora Mercandy before the final bell rang. The minute Elizabeth spotted Nora walking toward them, she waved. Nora's smile was timid but friendly.

Some of Nora's shyness seemed to vanish and her dark eyes sparkled when Elizabeth mentioned the tennis game with Lila. "When Jessica got home yesterday, that's all she could talk about," Elizabeth explained.

"Lila made a bet with me," Nora said. "I don't think she was very happy when I won it."

"What sort of bet?" Elizabeth asked curiously.

Before Nora could reply, Amy said, "I'm sorry I didn't get to meet you yesterday, Nora. I'm Amy Sutton."

"Hi," Nora said with a smile.

The final bell rang. As the three girls separated to take their assigned seats, Elizabeth said, "We'll meet you in the cafeteria for lunch, Nora. I remembered to bring the gym suit. . . just in case you want to clobber someone else in tennis today."

Lila overheard Elizabeth's words. She was still fuming about losing to the Mercandy witch the day before, but it didn't matter. She had a scheme to get even, and she had already set it in motion. Lila had made a point of seeing Ms. Pauley before class started. She told the teacher that an expensive cloisonné pen was missing from her purse. Now all she had to do was wait.

Ten minutes later the class was filling out a survey form. Nora removed the cloisonné pen from her book bag. This was the precise moment Lila had been waiting for. "That's my pen!" Lila shouted. Everyone followed Lila's gaze across the room. Nora Mercandy was holding a beautifully enameled pink and white ballpoint pen.

Nora's eyes went wide with surprise. She turned a deep shade of red when she suddenly realized that everyone was staring at her, and that Lila was accusing her of stealing her pen.

"Lila, what is this outburst all about?" Ms. Pauley asked, annoyed at the disturbance.

"She has my pen." Lila pointed her finger at Nora. "Ms. Pauley," Lila reminded the teacher, "remember just before class I told you that my pen was missing? Well, that's it. Nora Mercandy has it!"

"That's enough, Lila," Ms. Pauley warned.

Lila ignored the teacher. "My grandmother gave me that pen for my birthday. Anyone can see that Nora Mercandy is too poor to afford a pen that good."

"I said, that's enough, Lila!" To Nora, Ms. Pauley said, "Nora, would you mind stepping outside with me for a moment?"

Lila had been hoping Ms. Pauley would leave the room. She wasted no time. As soon as the door shut, she stood up beside her desk. "Listen, everybody. My cousin Janet lives on the same street as that weirdo. She really is a witch . . . we have proof."

"It's true," Ellen Riteman yelled. "The whole Mercandy family is crazy."

"Janet lives right next *door* to the Mercandy mansion," Lila explained to the class. "Ellen, tell them what Janet told us this morning."

Ellen half-rose in her chair. "Janet's mother has had a cat named Walter for over fifteen years. Last night Janet went into the backyard to call him inside. She heard Walter cry like he was in pain. She looked over into the Mercandys' backyard . . ." Ellen paused to get her audience's full attention. "Nora was out there holding Walter in her arms. When she saw Janet, she walked over to the fence. She held Walter up and gave him a strange look

. . . like she was casting a spell on him. Then she passed him through the fence to Janet."

Elizabeth felt herself becoming very angry. "So what's the point?"

Ellen shot Elizabeth a defiant look and said quickly, "This morning Janet's mother found Walter dead on the kitchen floor!"

The classroom was filled with gasps, and then a long silence. At last Amy said, "Maybe Walter ate some of Janet's cooking before he went to bed last night."

"That's not funny!" Lila shouted in anger. "My aunt had Walter for fifteen years. The Mercandy witch took one look at him and he was dead a few hours later. How can you explain that?"

"The cat was old," Elizabeth said sensibly. "It couldn't live forever."

Randy Masion, one of the smartest and shyest boys in the class, suddenly spoke up. "My uncle is an undertaker at the Todd Mortuary. Right after the Mercandys moved here, they called the mortuary and ordered two coffins. They wanted them delivered to their house! Right now there are two coffins sitting in the Mercandy attic!"

A long, stunned silence followed Randy's announcement. Finally Lila said dramatically, "For all we know, they might sleep in them. Nearly every night Janet's family notices strange lights flickering on and off in their attic."

Caroline Pearce said, "I was in the girls' room

yesterday when Nora walked in. I was brushing my hair. I was looking straight into the mirror when Nora came to stand beside me . . . but her reflection wasn't in the mirror!"

"Caroline," Elizabeth interrupted, "you know the mirror in the girls' room has been broken for weeks. Nora was probably standing in front of the section the janitor took out."

"I know what I saw," Caroline replied stubbornly.

Just then Ms. Pauley returned to the room—without Nora. "I've sent Nora to the vice-principal's office. I'm sure Mr. Edwards will want to speak to you too, Lila."

Lila gathered up her books and headed to the office. She was filled with confidence. She knew she was a good liar. Adults almost always believed her.

Nora was already seated in the outer office when Lila arrived. Lila took a seat across from her. She deliberately stared at the shy girl, trying to make her feel uneasy. Nora fidgeted nervously in her chair and tried to avoid Lila's piercing gaze. After a fifteen-minute wait the vice-principal's door opened. Mr. Edwards stepped outside, a serious look on his face. He held the door open as Lila and Nora entered his office. He waited until they were seated before he sat down behind his desk. "Now, I understand there is a problem concerning a pen." Nora and Lila both nodded solemnly.

"May I see the pen?" Mr. Edwards asked.

Nora quickly took the cloisonné pen from her notebook and handed it to the vice-principal. He asked Nora to tell him where she'd gotten the pen. As Nora started to explain about the tennis bet, Lila shouted, "She's lying!"

Mr. Edwards gave Lila a cold stare. "You'll have your chance to tell your side of the story, young lady. In the meantime, please do not interrupt again."

Lila could see that the vice-principal meant business, so she waited for her turn. When it came, she put on her sweetest look and denied again that there had been a bet. "The pen was a gift from my grandparents. Besides, I would never bet anything so valuable."

After listening carefully to both Nora and Lila, there was a long, uncomfortable silence while the vice-principal thought over the situation. When he had reached a decision, he spoke kindly to Lila. "I'm going to return your pen, Lila."

His words to Nora were stern. "Young lady, you are new to Sweet Valley. Perhaps you don't know that betting is forbidden in school. In any case, I don't know how you could have taken such an expensive item from anyone."

Nora had turned pale. Her lower lip started to

tremble as Mr. Edwards continued. "This has been an unfortunate incident. I hope I won't have to see either of you back in my office again."

As they left the office, Lila smiled innocently at the vice-principal. "Thank you for helping me get my pen back, Mr. Edwards," she said in a voice as sweet as syrup.

Not a word was exchanged between the two girls as they left for their first-period class. Nora concentrated on trying not to cry. Lila gave her a superior smile. No one could embarrass Lila Fowler and get away with it.

Before lunch Elizabeth and Amy saw Nora at her locker. They rushed over to find out what had happened in the vice-principal's office.

"Mr. Edwards believed Lila," Nora said after explaining how she had won the pen. "He acted very nice to her, and he warned me about making bets on school grounds. The bet wasn't even my idea." She choked back a sob.

"Don't worry, Nora. We believe you," Elizabeth said gently.

"I don't know why," Nora replied miserably. "Lila was so convincing, I almost believed her myself." Nora forced a shy smile with these last words.

"She's had a lot of practice lying. Lila Fowler's one of the most deceitful girls on earth." Amy gave Nora a sympathetic smile.

Elizabeth was about to tell Nora about some of the rumors that were being spread in homeroom, when they were interrupted by a tall goodlooking boy. It was Rick Hunter, the president of the seventh-grade class. Rick was one of the most popular boys at Sweet Valley Middle School.

"Are you Elizabeth or Jessica?" he asked with a grin.

"I'm Elizabeth." Elizabeth smiled back.

"Someday soon I'm going to be able to figure out which is which," Rick promised. To Nora he said, "You must be Nora Mercandy."

Nora gave a quiet nod.

"My name is Rick Hunter. I hear you're a terrific tennis player." Rick flashed a bright smile at Nora. "Maybe you'd like to play me some afternoon after school."

Nora flushed and stammered. "I—I . . . OK."

"Great!" Rick replied.

After Rick left, Amy gave an excited squeal. "Nora, I think he likes you! He's new in town, too, and one of the cutest boys in school!"

"Jessica has a mad crush on him," Elizabeth said.

A sudden thought crossed Elizabeth's mind. "Lila has a crush on him too. She's going to be angrier than ever when she finds out about your playing tennis with Rick Hunter."

"What do you think she'll do?"

"I don't know," Elizabeth answered, "but I'll bet she comes up with something."

"Remember, there's no betting on campus," Amy said with a laugh.

Even though Lila was sure she had taught Nora a lesson, she was not about to let up on her. The opportunity to get back at Nora a second time that day came during math—Lila's least favorite subject.

Ms. Wyler had warned the class the day before to be prepared for a quiz. Lila had spent so much time on the phone the previous night that she hadn't even thought of studying.

Lila wasn't even halfway through the test when she noticed Nora walk to the front of the room and deposit her paper in a plastic tray on the teacher's desk. She must be good, she thought. Then the idea came to her.

Lila continued to struggle with the long division until Ms. Wyler went to the back of the room to search for something in the supply cabinet. There wasn't much time! It was now or never. Lila's heart started to pound as she decided to make her move.

She walked casually to the teacher's desk and placed her quiz on the tray on top of Nora's. She glanced quickly to the rear of the room. The teacher was still busy. All of the students were hard at work. The few who had already completed the quiz were quietly reading or getting a head start on that day's homework.

Lila reached back into the tray and retrieved not only her own paper, but Nora's as well. She quickly erased Nora's name and in its place wrote "Lila Fowler." On her own paper she wrote Nora's name.

On the way back to her desk Lila's eyes darted about the room. No one was paying attention to her. She gave a sigh of relief as she sank into her seat. A sly smile played across her lips. Congratulations, Lila, she said to herself. Her smile widened. The Mercandy witch was going to get another good lesson. And soon.

In the basement of their home the Wakefield twins were busy practicing for their next ballet lesson. Stretching in time to the music, Elizabeth said, "I'm not saying the Unicorns have to like Nora, I just don't see why they have to be mean to her."

Jessica was executing a series of graceful turns. "She took Lila's pen. I don't blame Lila for telling Ms. Pauley. It was valuable. She wanted it back."

Elizabeth leaned back against the worn sofa that the twins used as a barre. "I believe Nora when she said she won the pen in a bet. Jess, I know the Unicorns. Once they decide not to like someone, they think up all kinds of rotten tricks to play on them."

Jessica ignored her twin and continued to dance.

A concerned frown creased Elizabeth's forehead. "Just don't let Lila talk you into anything that might hurt Nora."

Finally Jessica stopped and looked at her sister.

"Elizabeth, you always seem to think that I let Lila boss me around. I can make my own decisions."

"Then promise me you'll be nice to Nora," Elizabeth said quickly.

"I'll think about it," Jessica replied in a voice that was far from convincing.

Five

◇

"I can't wait to see her face when we get our quizzes back," Lila gasped. She was doubled over laughing.

Ellen fell back against the pillows on Lila's bed. Her voice was filled with admiration. "It took a lot of nerve to switch papers like that, Lila. I don't think I would have had the courage to do it."

Jessica Wakefield sat quietly in the window seat looking out onto the lush grounds of the Fowler home. A tennis court was located on the north side of the yard, and a swimming pool on the south side.

"How come you're not saying anything, Jessica?" There was a hint of irritation in Lila's voice.

Jessica said quickly, "I was just thinking how brave you were to switch the quiz papers."

Lila smiled broadly. "Yes, I was," she agreed, "and I have a few other plans in store for Nora Mercandy."

Jessica hesitated before replying. She was thinking about what Elizabeth had said. "Maybe we should just let her alone."

Mary Giaccio sat cross-legged on the floor. "We're only having fun." She tossed her brown hair behind her shoulder.

"That's right," said Lila. "We just want to have some fun with the Mercandy witch."

Jessica grinned. "Well, nobody likes having fun more than me."

Two days later Ms. Wyler passed back the graded math quizzes. Lila Fowler received an A; Nora Mercandy received a D. When the class started working on the day's assignment, Ms. Wyler called Nora up to her desk. Lila and Mary sneaked a glance at each other. They both smiled cunningly. Jessica deliberately avoided looking at either of her friends. She tried to concentrate on her assignment.

"Nora," Ms. Wyler said softly, "I realize you're new to our school. Possibly you haven't been taught long division yet."

Nora had been shocked when she saw the red D on her paper. She stared at the test in confusion. "No—I—" she stammered. "I'm usually very good at long division. I just don't know what happened, Ms. Wyler."

"I know from your previous school record that you are a good math student."

As she spoke, Nora inspected the paper closely. There must be some mistake, she suddenly realized. The figures were not in her handwriting! She glanced across the room and met Lila's dark, mocking eyes.

Lila could tell from the expression on Nora's face that she knew what had happened. But when tears started to spill down Nora's cheeks, Lila knew that Nora wouldn't dare point out the switched quizzes. As Nora returned to her desk, Lila hissed under her breath, "Serves you right, Mercandy Witch."

Ellen watched as Nora wiped her eyes with the back of her hand. When she reached her desk, she sat down in utter defeat. Ellen returned Lila's triumphant smile.

After math class Nora found Elizabeth and Amy waiting by her locker. "Hi," she said, hoping the two girls wouldn't be able to tell that she'd been crying.

But Elizabeth noticed right away. "What's wrong, Nora?" she asked, a look of concern crossing her face.

"Lila Fowler strikes again," Nora said. She held out her math quiz for Amy and Elizabeth to see. "She switched the names on our quizzes, and I ended up with a D."

"Nora, this is terrible!" Amy exclaimed. "What did Ms. Wyler say when you told her?"

Nora ignored Amy's question and busied herself with gathering the books she needed to take home with her that evening.

"You did tell Ms. Wyler, didn't you?" asked Elizabeth.

"No!" Nora exclaimed, slamming her locker shut. "I don't want any more trouble. I'll just stay as far away from Lila as I possibly can, and after a while all of this will end. I can bring up my math grade on the next quiz."

"But don't you see?" said Elizabeth. "If you don't tell on Lila now, what's to stop her from doing this sort of thing the next time—or even something worse?"

"I don't know . . . I guess I'll just have to take my chances." She started to walk down the hall with Amy and Elizabeth. "I just don't understand what I've done wrong. Lila can't be this upset about losing a tennis game. And practically everyone at this school treats me like a—a leper. Even when I walked into class on the very first day, I could feel a sort of hate." For the second time that afternoon tears filled Nora's brown eyes. "Why?"

Elizabeth and Amy exchanged uneasy glances. "You see, Nora," Amy began slowly, "a lot of people in town think your grandmother is a—"

"Is sort of weird," Elizabeth interrupted.

Nora's expression was both puzzled and surprised. "They think my grandmother is weird? Why?"

"Well . . ." Elizabeth hesitated. "You see, Nora, for years there have been rumors about your grandmother's mansion. And your grandparents seem like . . . hermits. No one ever sees them. So rumors started to circulate around town saying that they were . . . strange." Elizabeth couldn't bear to tell Nora that people said her grandmother was a witch who kept her husband chained in the attic.

"But—but that's crazy," Nora stammered. "I mean . . . it's true they always stay at home, but there's a good reason. I can explain—" Nora stopped in mid-sentence. A ray of hope came to her face. "What if I invited them over tomorrow to meet my grandmother?"

Nora could tell that Elizabeth and Amy were uncomfortable with the idea. " Don't you see," she insisted, her eyes shining, "if they met my grandmother, all of these silly rumors would stop."

Elizabeth felt a rush of pity at the hopeful look on Nora's face. "Well . . . maybe it wouldn't hurt to give it a try."

"But how are you going to get Lila over to your house?" Amy wanted to know.

"I can find a way," Elizabeth said decisively. "Nora, can we meet in your backyard at two o'clock tomorrow?"

Nora nodded. "I'll have to check with my grandparents, but I'm sure it will be all right."

"OK," Elizabeth said with a determined smile. "We'll see you tomorrow at two o'clock."

The three girls had reached the Mercandy mansion. Elizabeth and Amy waved good-bye to Nora as she walked up the stone path and disappeared within the darkness of the house.

Six

◇

On Saturday morning Elizabeth decided it was time to set Nora's plan into action. "Jess, what are you doing this afternoon?" she asked as she stretched across her twin's bed.

Jessica was in front of her dresser mirror lazily brushing her hair. She hadn't yet changed out of her pajamas. It took Jessica much longer to get moving in the morning than it did her twin. Elizabeth usually bounced out of bed alert and ready to meet the day. Jessica, on the other hand, tended to be somewhat grouchy for a good hour after she opened her eyes. Since she had been up less than fifteen minutes, she wasn't in one of her better moods. She gave a lazy shrug. "I'll probably go over to Lila's. She's invited some of the Unicorns over to watch the new video she bought last week."

"Would you do me a favor?" Elizabeth asked, using her most persuasive tone.

Jessica stopped brushing her hair. "That depends," she said suspiciously. "What do you want?"

"I need you to make certain that Lila and as many Unicorns as you can get are in the Mercandy backyard at two o'clock this afternoon."

Jessica whirled away from the mirror. "In the Mercandy backyard!" she exclaimed, her eyes wide. "Do you think we're crazy?"

"Nora wants to put a stop to all of the rumors about her grandparents and the Mercandy mansion."

Jessica blinked in disbelief. "How does she think she's going to do that?"

"I think she's going to introduce us to her grandmother," Elizabeth stated.

"I don't want to be introduced to any witch!" Jessica declared.

"Oh, come on, Jess," Elizabeth said. "She's probably a very nice old lady."

Jessica grunted. "I'll bet! She probably needs some meat for her Halloween dinner. I don't know about you, but I don't want to end up in any witches' brew!"

"Jessica, don't be ridiculous. Just bring Lila

and the other Unicorns to the Mercandys' backyard at two o'clock."

"What's in it for me?" Jessica asked.

"That's blackmail," said Elizabeth.

A slow smile spread across Jessica's face. "I
know."

Elizabeth knew her sister was weakening.
Whenever the two of them got to the what's-in-it-
for-me stage, it was usually just a matter of coming
up with a suitable bribe before Jessica gave in. In
this case Elizabeth knew the price would be high.

"I'll let you wear my new yellow sweater,"
Elizabeth suggested.

"Whenever I want to," Jessica added.

Elizabeth swallowed hard. This was going to
be worse than she'd expected. "OK."

"And you'll buy me a large popcorn the next
time we go to the movies—with extra butter," Jessica went on.

"With extra butter," Elizabeth echoed, sigh-
ing.

"And you'll set the dinner table for me for the
rest of the week, and —"

"Jessica . . ." Elizabeth warned, her voice ris-
ing.

"Elizabeth, I'm risking my life going over to
the Mercandys. The least you could do for me is a
couple of small favors." Jessica wore an expression
of angelic innocence.

"What else?" asked Elizabeth.

"And you'll do the dinner dishes tonight."

"Is that all?" Elizabeth asked sarcastically.

"Yes."

"Boy, you sure are pushing it. My new yellow sweater, setting the table, the dishes. . ."

"And the popcorn," Jessica finished. "Don't forget about the popcorn."

"Oh, all right," said Elizabeth. "All right to all of it. But promise you'll be there."

Jessica promised, crossing her heart as she did.

At one o'clock Jessica stood on the Fowlers' front porch. A rather tired and annoyed-looking maid answered the door. "Just head toward the noise," she said.

Jessica tried not to smile. Even she had to admit that the music coming out of Lila's room was pretty loud. She and Elizabeth were never allowed to play music that could be heard outside their bedrooms.

When Jessica reached Lila's spacious room, she saw that Ellen Riteman, Tamara Chase, and Kimberly Haver had already arrived. The four girls were dancing to a rock video on Lila's color TV. Jessica joined them. A few minutes later Janet Howell walked in just as the video ended.

"Isn't that the greatest song?" Lila asked as

the girls collapsed on the floor. "My father picked it up on a business trip in London."

"Oh," Jessica said, "then your father will be here for your Halloween party?"

"No, he left again this morning. This time he's in New York." Lila shrugged and added with a broad smile, "But he promised me an expensive gift when he comes back next week."

"Do you ever miss not having your parents around?" Jessica asked. She couldn't imagine what the Wakefield home would be like without her mother or father.

"I missed my mother when she first moved away," Lila admitted reluctantly. "But I get to visit her for two weeks every summer. My father stops by for a few days, sometimes even for a week at a time, between business trips." Lila started looking through her video collection. "Once you get used to it, it's sort of neat not having parents around to breathe down your neck."

"Yeah," Kimberly agreed. "I sometimes wish my parents would take a long vacation."

Lila removed a videotape from its case and plopped down on one of the overstuffed pillows on the floor. "I'll show this one next, but first I want to tell you about an idea I have for a new club."

"A new club?" Jessica said in surprise. "What's wrong with the Unicorn Club?"

Lila laughed and tossed her gleaming brown hair. "Nothing. I mean in addition to the Unicorns. This is what happened. Last week Janet and I went to a Sweet Valley High football game with my aunt and uncle."

"My brother is on the varsity team," Ellen interrupted proudly.

"At high school games they have cheerleaders," Lila explained. "I thought maybe we could start something like that at Sweet Valley Middle School for basketball season. We could even think up our own cheers."

The idea appealed to Jessica immediately. "We could make pom-poms in our school colors and twirl batons! I'm a good dancer; I could make up some routines . . ." The other girls were nodding and murmuring enthusiastically.

Lila smiled. She was glad to see that her friends were as excited about her idea as she was. "I thought we could call ourselves the Boosters."

"We'll probably have to get permission from one of the teachers," said Ellen.

"Don't worry," Lila assured her. "I'll talk to Ms. Langberg. I'm sure she'll like the idea."

After some more discussion about the new club, the conversation turned back to Lila's Halloween party.

"So, only the servants will be here next Friday night?" Ellen asked eagerly.

"Yes," Lila replied. "But I think we need to get together with the other Unicorns before then to make some special plans."

"What do you have in mind?" asked Jessica.

"I'm not sure, but I do know I want us to play a trick on Nora Mercandy. Something she'll remember every Halloween for the rest of her life."

"Maybe we can 'decorate' the Mercandy mansion," Tamara said, picking up on Lila's mood.

"We could put toilet paper on all of the trees and bushes," Ellen piped up.

Lila's eyes gleamed with pleasure at the thought of tormenting Nora. "We could, only I want to do more than just spread some paper around. That's kid stuff. Maybe we should ask some of the boys and see if they have any ideas. Maybe we should invite Nora to my party so we can really make a fool of her."

"Speaking of Nora Mercandy, I have a message to deliver from her," Jessica said nervously.

The five other girls sat up straight.

"Elizabeth told me this morning that Nora wants us to meet her in her backyard this afternoon."

Tamara's eyes were wide with disbelief. "In the Mercandy backyard! I wouldn't set foot on that property . . . I mean, who knows what could happen?"

Lila was immediately suspicious. "Why does she want us there?"

Jessica started to smile. "Elizabeth told Nora that people were treating her badly because they thought her grandparents were hermits."

"*Hermits?*" The Unicorns screeched in laughter. Lila was the first to calm down. "Why didn't Elizabeth tell her the truth?"

"Nora wants to prove that her grandparents are normal old people," Jessica continued, ignoring Lila's question. "She invited all the Unicorns over to her house at two o'clock."

Ellen glanced at her watch. "That's only twenty minutes from now."

"I think we should go," Janet said.

Lila stared at her cousin as if she were a creature from outer space. "You can't be serious!"

"I am serious," Janet assured Lila. Her eyes began to sparkle. "I'd like to see what a real witch looks like in person."

"But it could be dangerous," Lila reminded her.

"Even if old lady Mercandy is a witch, she's an *old* witch," Kimberly said. "We could outrun her if we had to."

"A witch can work magic and cast spells," Lila said. "What if she wants to get back at me for some of the things I've done to Nora?" Her expression changed. "Besides," she said huffily, "who does Nora Mercandy think she is anyway . . . inviting the *Unicorns* to her house? We're a special club. We don't go to just anybody's house."

The other Unicorns nodded in agreement. Jessica, thinking of her promise to Elizabeth—not to mention the yellow sweater, the popcorn, and the chores she wouldn't have to do—finally said, "I still have to admit that I am a little curious. Aren't you, Lila?"

Lila shrugged. "I guess . . . maybe a little."

"Why don't we just sneak around the back of the house and peek through the fence?" Ellen suggested.

After a long pause Lila nodded her approval. "OK, let's go!"

The Unicorns hurried out of the Fowler house and along the streets of Sweet Valley that led to the Mercandy mansion. Along the way they passed Bruce Patman riding his bicycle. He stopped and grinned at them.

"Where is the Unicorn Club going today?" Bruce asked.

"To the Mercandy mansion," Jessica was quick to inform him.

Bruce looked surprised. "You're kidding. You're going to the witch's house?"

The girls quickly explained the situation. Bruce whistled loudly. "You really think she's going to introduce you to old lady Mercandy? I've never seen a witch before . . . I'm coming too!"

The girls were delighted. Bruce Patman was

one of the boys they talked about the most. More than once they had rated him the cutest seventh grader in Sweet Valley.

As soon as they came near the Mercandy mansion, the six girls and Bruce automatically slowed their pace and lowered their voices. They walked around to the backyard, following the high iron fence surrounding the entire Mercandy property. There was a space of about six inches between each iron bar, which made it easy to see into the backyard, even through the overgrown shrubbery.

The seven leaned their heads against the iron fence and silently surveyed the situation. The yard was overrun with weeds and untended fruit trees and shade trees. A table had been set up beneath a giant gnarled oak tree. Elizabeth and Amy were busy placing paper plates, glasses, and napkins on the table.

Lila gave a snort of contempt. "So, the witch thinks she's going to have a Saturday afternoon tea party."

"Shhh . . ." Janet warned her cousin. "Here she comes." The Unicorns, along with Bruce Patman, crouched down behind the bushes, where they couldn't be seen.

The screen door on the back porch slammed shut. Nora carried a large pitcher of punch which she set down in the center of the table. She gave a guarded smile to Elizabeth and Amy. "Do you think they'll come?" she asked.

"Don't worry, Nora," Elizabeth said, "it's not quite two o'clock yet. They'll be here."

"I'll go get the cookies," Nora said, returning to the house. When Nora had disappeared inside the mansion, the Unicorns and Bruce crept closer to the open iron gate.

"Lizzie," Jessica called in a hushed voice, "is it really safe to come inside?"

Elizabeth gave a sigh of relief when she heard her sister's voice. She had been afraid the Unicorns wouldn't show up. "Of course it's safe," she replied.

Elizabeth watched as the Unicorns took several cautious steps inside the backyard. Trailing behind with equal caution was Bruce Patman.

"Have you seen old lady Mercandy yet?" Lila asked.

"Not yet," Amy answered.

"Nora went to get some cookies that her grandmother had baked. She said she was going to ask her grandmother to come out as soon as everyone arrived," Elizabeth said.

Lila and the other Unicorns looked at one another. They were now well inside the Mercandy backyard. The screen door opened and Nora came out carrying a tray loaded with freshly baked cookies. She stopped when she saw the Unicorns.

It was clear to everyone that she was very nervous. She placed the tray on the table. With a tentative smile she managed to get out a weak hello. Although the hello was intended for everyone in general, Nora's eyes never left Lila's face. She knew that it was Lila who would decide the outcome of today's meeting.

"So, where's old lady Mercandy?" Lila demanded. If she was nervous, she didn't show it.

"My grandmother will be out in a minute," Nora replied. "Would you like some cookies and punch first?"

"How do we know you haven't poisoned them?" Ellen's eyes narrowed with suspicion.

Elizabeth laughed and took a cookie. "Don't be silly, Ellen. Here." She passed the tray to Amy. "Amy and I will have one first."

As Bruce and Lila reached for the tray, the screen door suddenly burst wide open. Standing in the doorway was a tall man in a black suit. His white hair stuck out wildly in all directions, and his face was ghostly pale. He walked stiffly as he took a step forward. In a deep, menacing voice he mumbled one word over and over again. "Nor . . . Nor . . . Nor . . ."

Still walking stiffly, he moved toward the children with slow, unbalanced steps.

"It's a zombie!" Lila screamed.

The tray of cookies that Amy was holding crashed to the ground.

"It *is* a zombie!" Bruce yelled. "Let's get out of here!" As he spoke, Bruce dashed toward the back gate. All six Unicorns were right behind him.

Elizabeth and Amy were holding on to each other, but they didn't move. They just kept staring at the strange man. Nora, realizing that her chances to settle things with the Unicorns had been ruined, burst into tears. "You'd better leave now," she sobbed.

Elizabeth and Amy turned and rushed out of the yard. Behind them they could still hear the man mumbling, "Nor . . . Nor . . . Nor . . ."

Seven

◇

A zombie at the Mercandy mansion! Between the Unicorns, Bruce Patman, and Caroline Pearce, the news spread across town like wildfire.

In homeroom on Monday morning it was clear to Nora that there wasn't a single student who didn't look at her strangely or avoid her altogether. To make matters worse, for some reason Elizabeth and Amy weren't in class.

At lunchtime Nora sat alone in the cafeteria. She kept her eyes lowered, but she couldn't help noticing the Unicorn table and the crowd of people gathered around it.

"He looked just like the Frankenstein monster," Ellen was saying for about the hundredth time that day.

"He walked straight toward us and he kept

mumbling one word over and over again," Lila was telling Mary Giaccio. "It sounded like 'murder, murder, murder.'"

Mary gasped in horror, as did everyone else who had gathered around to hear what had scared the Unicorns at the Mercandy mansion. The story went from table to table, and the more it was repeated, the more it changed and grew. By the end of the lunch period there were rumors flying around Sweet Valley Middle School that a monster with a knife had tried to kill the Unicorns.

Lila, Jessica, and Ellen left the cafeteria ten minutes early to walk to gym class. That gave them plenty of time to talk more about the "zombie." "I get the creeps every time I think of it," Ellen said.

"Do you think he was a real zombie?" Jessica asked.

"I don't know, but he was weird," Lila said. "What really makes me mad," she added, "is that Nora wanted to get us to the Mercandy mansion just so she could scare us."

"That *was* mean of her," Ellen said. "I think we should show her she can't go around trying to scare anybody in the Unicorn Club."

"We can't let anyone make us look bad," Jessica said in a determined voice.

Ellen gave Lila a knowing smile. "I get the feeling you have something up your sleeve, Lila."

Lila's eyes narrowed and a crafty smile spread

across her face. "Yes, I do. I have an idea that's going to pay off for all the Unicorns. What we need is a slave . . . and I think that Nora would make the perfect one." Before they reached the gym, Lila explained exactly what she was going to do.

Nora had already changed into her gym clothes when the other girls in the class started to drift into the locker room. Again Nora wondered where Elizabeth and Amy were. She sat alone on the small wooden bench in front of her locker. She was afraid to speak to anyone, and everyone around her acted as if she were invisible.

Lila soon changed that. She sauntered down the narrow aisle between the long rows of lockers and stopped in front of Nora. Then she folded her arms and gave Nora a long, cold stare. "The Unicorns would like to have a little talk with you right after class."

Nora's heart started to pound. "Wh-what about?" she stammered.

"We'll let you know after class. Meet us at the front door of the gym," Lila ordered.

For the next half hour the girls played volleyball. Nora, usually a good athlete, couldn't concentrate on the game. She couldn't understand where Elizabeth and Amy could have disappeared to. She hoped they weren't purposely avoiding her. When the bell rang, Nora started to feel desperate. She quickly showered, dressed, grabbed her books, and made a dash for the door.

Standing in the doorway she saw a welcome sight. Nora smiled for the first time that day. "Elizabeth—"

"I'm Jessica," Jessica informed her coldly. She watched Nora's smile fade before she continued. "Lila told you to wait here."

"Yes, but . . ."

"Just don't run off to study hall before she gets here," Jessica warned. "We want to talk to you."

Nora sighed, her shoulders sagging. She felt helpless. When Lila and Ellen arrived, she just stood there, frozen. The three girls surrounded her.

Lila, as usual, took charge. "We know you invited us to your house on Saturday just to scare us."

"That's not true," Nora protested.

"Shut up and listen to Lila!" Ellen said.

Lila smiled at Ellen before she turned her attention back to Nora. "To pay for the way you treated us on Saturday, you're going to run an errand for us this afternoon."

"What kind of errand?" Nora asked in a small voice.

"The Unicorns love cookies," said Lila. "Our favorites are the giant chocolate chips from the Some Crumb Bakery on Yale Avenue. During study hall you're to go over there and buy us a dozen chocolate chip cookies."

"And get them back here before study hall's over," Ellen piped up. "We want to have plenty of time to enjoy them."

Nora's eyes went wide with concern. "But students aren't allowed to leave the school grounds during study hall," she said.

"No kidding," Ellen said sarcastically.

"What if I get caught? I could really get in trouble."

Lila shrugged. "That's the chance you have to take."

Nora swallowed hard. It took all of her courage to look straight at Lila. "You can't order me around, Lila."

"Yes, I can," Lila replied confidently. "If you don't follow my instructions, tomorrow you're going to be in trouble anyway. With Mr. Edwards again."

"I haven't done anything. How can you get me in trouble?"

Lila gave Nora a look as cold as ice. "I know the combination to your locker. If you don't do what the Unicorns ask, then my wallet is going to be found inside it. Ellen and Jessica will tell Mr. Edwards they saw you take the wallet from my purse."

Nora gasped. She knew that the vice-principal wouldn't take her word against two eye-witnesses. She had to do whatever the Unicorns asked her to.

"But . . . I don't have any money," she said desperately.

"We know," Lila said haughtily. She opened her purse and shoved a five-dollar bill into Nora's palm. "Take this and have the cookies back here by the end of study hall." With that Lila turned on her heel and marched off. The other Unicorns were close behind her.

At the start of study hall Nora asked for permission to go to the bathroom. She slipped out and hurried off the school grounds by way of the football field. She ran several blocks across town to the Some Crumb Bakery and she managed to sneak back into the auditorium with twenty minutes left in the period.

As she walked down the aisle to her seat, Nora stopped at the row where the Unicorns were waiting. Her hands trembled as she placed the bag of cookies on the small folding desk in front of Lila.

"Well done, slave." Lila spoke like a queen. "We'll give you more orders tomorrow. You're excused now."

Nora headed shakily to her seat. Her stomach churned with fear. What might the Unicorns think up for her next? She opened her math book and looked around desperately for Elizabeth and Amy. They were still nowhere to be found. Nora was sure now that they had abandoned her. She felt completely alone.

Eight

◇

At seven-thirty that evening the Wakefields were gathered in the living room of their split-level ranch house. Mr. Wakefield and Steven were watching a football game on TV, Mrs. Wakefield was curled up on the couch reading a novel, and the twins were busy putting finishing touches on their Halloween costumes.

Jessica slipped a red and yellow plastic lei around her neck. In a halter top and grass skirt, she began to hula around the living room.

"Oh, brother," Steven hooted. "Now I never want to go to Hawaii."

"I think she looks cute," Mrs. Wakefield said, coming to Jessica's defense.

Jessica ignored Steven. "Thank you, Mom,"

said Jessica. "I bet Lila, Ellen, and I will win the ribbons for prettiest costume this year."

"All three of you are going to be hula girls? You'd better hope they're giving out booby prizes." Steven gave his sister a teasing grin.

Jessica kicked her brother lightly on the shin. "I'd rather be a hula dancer than the Creature from the Black Lagoon."

"Are you going to model your costume for us?" Mr. Wakefield asked Elizabeth.

"I will, Dad, just as soon as I'm finished." Elizabeth was busy sewing a big bright button on the front of a clown suit.

"Jessica, did you give Nora my message today?"

"What message?" Jessica pretended not to know what her twin was talking about.

"I told you this morning to tell Nora that I'd see her tomorrow," Elizabeth replied in an annoyed voice. "I wanted you to let her know why Amy and I wouldn't be around today."

"Have you been doing something special at school, dear?" Mrs. Wakefield asked.

"Yes, Julie and Amy and I were busy finishing up the newest issue of *The Sweet Valley Sixers*. It comes out at the end of every month. We've been working on it during homeroom, lunch, gym, and study hall." Elizabeth turned her attention back to Jessica. "I hope the Unicorns haven't been giving Nora a hard time."

Jessica shrugged. "You can't expect us to just forget that weird zombie coming at us, can you? She got us over to her house on Saturday just to scare us."

"That's not true," Elizabeth said. "She wanted to try to make friends with you."

"Friends!" Jessica sniffed. "Who wants to be friends with a witch?" She turned away and rushed out of the room, her grass skirt swishing as she walked.

The next day at lunchtime Elizabeth and Amy waited for Nora at their usual table in the cafeteria. They waved her over as soon as they saw her.

Nora walked slowly to the table and gave them an uncertain smile. "Hi . . . I—I—thought you both decided not to be friends with me anymore. Not after what happened last Saturday."

"We know that wasn't your fault, Nora," Elizabeth assured her. "Amy and I haven't been around because we've been busy finishing the sixth-grade newspaper. I told Jess to tell you where we were."

Nora sighed. "Well, she didn't."

"I know," Elizabeth replied. "And I got the feeling after talking to her last night that the Unicorns are bothering you again."

"They treat me like a slave," Nora said sadly. Both Amy and Elizabeth listened as she filled them in on all that had happened the past two days. Not only had they sent her on errands, that morning in social studies Lila had ordered Nora to make extra copies of the previous night's math homework for Lila, Jessica, and Ellen to use. When she finished explaining, Nora said to Elizabeth, "It's hard to believe that you and Jessica can be so different."

Elizabeth looked embarrassed. She was usually quick to defend her sister, but not this time. "I'm really sorry, Nora. I'm just furious at Jessica. If my parents ever found out about this, she'd be grounded for a month. Maybe we can think of some way to stop the Unicorns from bugging you so much."

Elizabeth had thought about confronting Jessica about the Unicorns' mean treatment of Nora. But Elizabeth knew from experience that when Jessica was backed into a corner, she fought back with all her might. But if she were left alone, Jessica grew tired of most things pretty quickly.

Maybe that was it. Maybe instead of fighting against the Unicorns, it would be better if Nora kept doing whatever they asked. They got bored quickly. With Halloween only a few days away, maybe Lila Fowler would be so caught up with planning her party, she'd forget all about her "slave."

But Elizabeth didn't know that the Unicorns had a big surprise in store for Nora Mercandy.

Nine

◇

The following morning Nora's heart sank as she saw Lila, Jessica, and Ellen waiting for her in the hallway outside homeroom. Oh, no, she thought, another order. Nora tried to walk past them, but the Unicorn threesome blocked the way.

Lila gave her a friendly smile. "Nora," she said lightly, "we want to talk to you for a minute, please. We want you to know how sorry we are for the way we've treated you." She sounded almost pleading.

"Wh—what did you say?" Nora's shock was evident from the expression on her face.

Lila repeated with her sweetest smile, "I said that we're sorry for the way we've been acting."

Nora studied Lila carefully. The light brown

eyes and the friendly smile seemed sincere. But how could they be? Nora grew even more puzzled when Lila said, "The Unicorns had a meeting last night. We decided that what happened last Saturday wasn't your fault. We've decided we would like you to be our friend."

Nora was speechless. Her eyes slowly and carefully searched the face of each girl. Her gaze was returned by three warm smiles. Slowly Nora turned and entered homeroom, too shocked to say a word to anyone.

At lunchtime Elizabeth and Amy waited for Nora at their usual lunch table. But as she looked around the crowded cafeteria, Amy suddenly gasped. "I don't believe it!"

Elizabeth's eyes widened in surprise. Nora Mercandy was surrounded by Unicorns. She was sitting at the Unicorn table between Lila and Jessica. The girls were talking and laughing together. From where Elizabeth and Amy sat, it appeared that Nora had found a whole new group of best friends.

"*You* can't believe it!" Elizabeth exclaimed. "It's . . . it's impossible! Something must be wrong. . . ."

Seated at the Unicorn table, Nora felt very nervous and uncomfortable. She glanced over at Elizabeth and Amy. She wished she could join them, but she didn't want to make the Unicorns angry at her again. She was still suspicious, but she had to admit they were being nice.

"And after school today we're going to the Dairi Burger for a Coke," Lila said. "We'd love you to join us."

"The Dairi Burger?" Nora repeated.

"All the really neat kids hang out there," said Jessica.

"It will be my treat," Lila offered. Her brown eyes were warm and friendly. She smiled at Nora. For the first time since meeting her, Nora realized that Lila was rather pretty.

The Unicorns didn't let Nora out of their sight for a single moment, and they were nice to her for the entire day. Even though she and Elizabeth exchanged a quick hello during gym class, they couldn't talk privately.

At the Dairi Burger Nora sat awkwardly amid a large group of Unicorns including lots of seventh- and eighth-grade girls.

Nora was starting to relax a little, but when she saw Bruce Patman coming toward the Unicorn table, she drew in a quick breath. She hoped he wouldn't say anything nasty about the scene in her backyard the previous Saturday.

To Nora's amazed relief, Bruce grinned at her. "Hi, Nora," he said in a warm, friendly voice. "I guess I should tell you I'm sorry about rushing off the other day."

Nora stared at Bruce. He sounded really sincere. She forced herself to say in a light voice, "That's . . . OK."

"Has Lila invited you to her Halloween party yet?" Bruce asked.

"Er . . . no." Nora felt her face turning red.

"I was just about to ask you, Nora." Lila smiled. "I'm having a Halloween costume party at my house at seven-thirty tomorrow night. A lot of kids from school and all of the Unicorns will be there. I hope you can come too."

"Well . . . I don't know," Nora hesitated.

"Elizabeth and Amy will be there," Jessica was quick to add.

"It's going to be a great party," Lila promised.

"Thank you, Lila. I'll have to ask my grandparents. It sounds like fun," Nora said politely.

"What kind of costume are you planning to wear tomorrow, Nora?" asked Jessica.

"I don't know," Nora answered. "At my other school we didn't dress up on Halloween. I guess I'll see what kind of old clothes I can find at my grandparents' house."

"I have an idea," Lila said. "Why don't you come as a witch? That would show everybody you didn't take all the teasing seriously."

"I could," Nora said slowly. "I'll see."

After they had ordered sundaes, Nora excused herself to go to the bathroom. As soon as she was out of sight, the Unicorns doubled over laughing. Janet Howell, the club president, was the first to recover. "That stupid witch really believes we're her friends."

"Just wait until tomorrow night," Bruce snickered.

"Is she in for a surprise!" Jessica spoke through a fit of giggles.

Lila's sly expression had returned. "I can't wait to get a look at her face when she finds out this was just a trick to get her away from her house and to make a fool of her for coming dressed as herself, a witch!"

"Just make certain she stays at your party for at least half an hour," Bruce said. "It will take us that long to really do a job on the Mercandy mansion."

Jessica asked curiously, "What are you planning to do exactly?"

"Quiet!" Bruce warned. "We'll tell you later. Here she comes!"

When Nora returned to the table, there was an uncomfortable silence. Finally Bruce waved at all the girls. "See you tomorrow."

"Yes, tomorrow," Nora said to Bruce with a wink. "It's going to be the best Halloween ever!"

Ten

◇

There was excitement in the air when Jessica and Elizabeth woke up the next morning. Halloween had arrived at last! The twins took an extra long time in front of their dresser mirrors applying makeup and getting into their costumes.

After slipping into the polka-dotted clown outfit she had worked on for days, Elizabeth applied two big round spots of rouge to her already rosy cheeks. She covered her blond hair with a curly red wig made of yarn. The finishing touch was a gigantic red rubber nose. She laughed aloud as she inspected herself in the floor-length mirror attached to her door to the twins' shared bathroom.

Jessica stood beside Elizabeth and admired

her own costume. She had put on lots of Pan-Cake makeup, long false eyelashes, and wore a black wig that hung to her waist. Dressed in the grass skirt, halter top, and flowered lei, she did a few hula steps in front of the mirror.

When they appeared downstairs, Steven almost choked on a spoonful of cereal. When he was finally able to speak, he said, "Boy, do you two look stupid."

Mrs. Wakefield smiled at both girls. "You both look adorable," she said, giving Elizabeth's rubber nose an affectionate squeeze.

Mr. Wakefield grinned at his daughters. "I think you've done a great job on your costumes."

Jessica was often teased by her family for having an enormous appetite. On special days such as this one, she ate even more than usual. This morning her plate was piled high with a huge serving of scrambled eggs, bacon, and a piece of toast smothered with grape jelly. She gave a toss of her black wig and lifted a forkful of eggs to her mouth. At that instant one of her false eyelashes dropped onto her toast and sank into the sticky jelly.

Steven almost choked for a second time. Even Elizabeth and her parents couldn't keep from laughing. Jessica angrily retrieved the eyelash. Holding it delicately between her thumb and forefinger, she marched upstairs to wash and repair it.

On the way to school Jessica was met by her

two hula partners, Lila and Ellen. The trio swayed all the way to hula music blaring from Lila's cassette player.

Meanwhile Elizabeth stopped by Amy's house. Amy opened the front door wearing a clown costume nearly identical to Elizabeth's. Elizabeth giggled. "I feel like I have another twin."

Although it was awkward walking in the clown suits, Elizabeth and Amy hurried along the streets of Sweet Valley. Their classmates were dressed in all sorts of outrageous costumes. Some of them were easy to identify, while others were impossible to recognize in their makeup or masks.

Elizabeth and Amy gasped when they saw Nora Mercandy. She looked like a real witch! Her costume consisted of a pointed black hat, stringy black and gray hair, a long black dress, and buckled black shoes. It was the makeup that made Nora look truly grotesque. Her face was pure white with black paint around her eyes. Her hands were also painted white, and long animallike claws hung at the ends of her fingers.

"Nora . . ." Elizabeth hesitated. She wasn't quite sure if she was talking to Nora or to a real witch. For just an instant she thought of all the rumors about the Mercandys.

"Hi, Elizabeth; hi, Amy," Nora called. "I'm sorry I didn't get to talk to you yesterday."

"That's OK," Elizabeth replied.

"I can't figure out why the Unicorns were so nice to me all of a sudden," Nora said, still puzzled. The hideous wrinkled white face broke into a smile. "Lila even invited me to her party tonight."

Elizabeth smiled at Nora. "Maybe they finally realized how nice you really are. Anyway," she added, "I'm glad you'll be at the party."

"Thanks . . . so am I," Nora admitted shyly.

The bell for homeroom rang. Together the two clowns and the horrible-looking witch hurried across the school grounds to class.

When Ms. Pauley entered her homeroom, no one even noticed. Students were all over the room checking out one another's costumes. Charlie Cashman was dressed like a pirate. He was racing around waving a silver cardboard sword over his head. Someone dressed as King Kong was standing on a desk grunting and pounding his hairy chest. A tramp carrying a knapsack over his shoulder pretended to try to catch King Kong. Above the din was the hula music coming from Lila's cassette player.

Elizabeth and Amy came into the class and found their seats. They were followed by Nora. When Nora entered the room, Lila turned off her hula music and stared. Suddenly the room became silent. All eyes followed Nora as she walked to her desk.

Nora Mercandy had come dressed as exactly what everyone had said she was—an evil witch!

Even Ms. Pauley was impressed by Nora's costume. "That's the most authentic-looking witch's outfit I believe I've ever seen, Nora."

Nora replied with a shy "Thank you."

Ms. Pauley turned her attention to the entire class. "I know it's difficult to sit quietly in your seats on Halloween." A slow smile spread across the teacher's face. "Therefore, I think I won't ask you to stay in your seats this morning."

The room was filled with cheers. King Kong pounded his chest in appreciation, and Charlie Cashman pounded the tramp's head with his cardboard sword. The Sweet Valley Middle School Halloween celebration had begun!

At lunchtime the Unicorns again insisted that Nora join them at their table.

"That's really a spooky costume, Nora," Jessica said in an admiring tone.

"How did you ever put it together?" Lila asked.

Nora shrugged. "I talked to my grandmother. She looked around in the attic and came up with this outfit just as you suggested."

The Unicorns exchanged silent but curious glances. Why would anyone have such realistic-looking witch's clothes in their attic unless . . . "You're coming to my party tonight, aren't you?"- Lila asked.

"Yes, if I'm still invited," Nora said shyly.

"Of course," Lila insisted. "It just wouldn't be the same without you!"

Nora didn't notice the sly smile that crossed Lila's face as she spoke.

Lila Fowler's Halloween party started at seven-thirty. Many of the sixth graders from Sweet Valley Middle School had been invited, along with a number of seventh and eighth graders. Of course, all the Unicorns were there.

Lila walked from group to group and did her best to make everyone feel honored that they had been invited to her party. From time to time she adjusted the blue ribbon she had won in Ms. Pauley's class so that everyone would notice. Just as Jessica had predicted, she, Ellen, and Lila had won prizes for the prettiest costumes.

Lila smoothed down her dark wig as she approached Rick Hunter and some of his seventh-grade friends. "I'm *so* delighted you could come to my party, Rick," Lila said in her most sophisticated voice. She batted her fake eyelashes, hoping they made her look sexy.

"Do you have something in your eye, Lila?" Rick asked.

"Er . . . no," Lila replied. She decided it was time to change the subject. "Rick," Lila said coyly, "you know I have my own private tennis court in the backyard. I wish you'd come over and play sometime."

"Thanks, Lila, maybe I will." Rick looked around the enormous living room. "Speaking of tennis, I was wondering if Nora Mercandy is here."

Lila was definitely not happy with the way the conversation was going. "She should be here any minute now," she sniffed.

Rick nodded. "I'll just keep an eye out for her. I want to set up a tennis date with her too."

Annoyed, Lila moved toward some of her Unicorn friends. At least they would appreciate her. She sidled up to Ellen, Janet, and Jessica.

"Guess what?" Lila said. "I talked to Ms. Langberg today. She gave us permission to organize the Booster Club."

"Good!" Jessica replied eagerly. "I can hardly wait. I have some great ideas for cheerleading routines."

"Well, there's a catch," Lila added with a frown. "Ms. Langberg said we would have to hold tryouts for the club. She said they would have to be open to anyone who's interested."

"Oh . . ." Both Ellen and Janet groaned in disappointment.

Jessica shrugged. "So what's the big deal? The tryouts can be open to everyone." Her dimple deepened in a sly smile. "That doesn't mean we have to choose just anyone. . . ."

"That's right," Ellen said with a grin. "We

can't help it if we just happen to choose our best friends."

"I think we should try to get as many Unicorns as possible into the Boosters," said Janet.

"Ms. Langberg suggested that we make some posters. We're supposed to hang them around school so that everybody will know when the tryouts are. We can make them small." Lila giggled.

Just then Ellen spotted Ken Matthews. "Look at Ken," she said in a whisper. "He's really cute—it's too bad he's so short." The Unicorns spent a lot of time rating various boys from Sweet Valley.

"I think he's a total loser," said Jessica. "He's practically a midget."

"When are Bruce and Charlie going to sneak away from the party?" Ellen asked.

"I'm not sure," Lila replied. "Just remember, we have to keep the witch busy for a half hour or so, so she won't notice when they leave. Wait till she sees what they do to her house! Just then Lila saw the maid ushering Nora Mercandy into the room. With a false smile Lila waved at Nora.

Nora walked slowly over to where the small group of Unicorns had gathered in the center of the living room. She was wearing her witch's costume.

"This is really a beautiful house, Lila," she told her hostess politely.

Lila shrugged. "Yes, I know. My father makes a lot of money."

Across the room Nora spotted Elizabeth and Amy, still in their clown costumes. She waved and started to walk toward them, when Jessica took her by the arm and steered her in another direction.

Jessica flashed her sweetest smile. "Come with me, Nora. I'll show you where the food is."

Reluctantly Nora followed Jessica into the dining room.

Elizabeth had taken off her rubber clown nose so that she could manage to drink a glass of punch without spilling it. "I wonder what Bruce and Charlie are whispering about," she said to Amy.

Amy followed Elizabeth's gaze. The two boys were soon joined by Jerry McAllister. All three suddenly burst into laughter.

"Knowing those guys, I'll bet they're up to something," Amy said.

Just then the three boys slipped quietly away from the crowded living room.

In the dining room Jessica received a thumbs-up signal from Lila. This meant that Bruce and his friends were on their way to the Mercandy mansion. Jessica's attitude toward Nora changed abruptly. "So, Nora, how have you enjoyed yourself so far this evening?" she asked harshly.

Nora blinked. "Everything has been . . . very nice. I'm glad Lila invited me."

"We're sure glad you came dressed as yourself, Mercandy Witch," Ellen said with a voice full of sarcasm.

"Yes," Lila continued loudly, "having a *genuine and ugly* witch come to your Halloween party sort of adds to the fun." Some of the other guests turned around and stared. A few of them snickered.

Nora just stared at the Unicorns. They had turned against her again! This had all been a trick to get her to Lila's party and make fun of her . . . but why? Were they going to do something terrible to her? Tears sprang to her eyes. She had to see Elizabeth and Amy. She turned and started into the living room. Behind her Jessica, Lila, and Ellen were still laughing.

Nora got as far as the hallway and stopped short. She overheard Tamara Chase talking to Janet Howell and two other eighth-grade Unicorns. "Some of the boys just left to take care of the Mercandy mansion. They've got rotten eggs, toilet paper, spray paint, and loads of other stuff." Tamara and the girls broke into peals of laughter.

So that was it! They weren't going to hurt her. It was her home. Her grandparents.

Suddenly Nora could stand no more. She marched into the dining room. Trembling with rage, her cries could be heard throughout the Fowler house. "I hate you, Lila! I hate all of you!"

She whirled around and dashed out the front door.

There was a stunned silence while everyone tried to figure out what had happened. Elizabeth made her way toward Jessica. "What have you done to her now?" she demanded.

"What are you blaming me for?" Jessica asked. "You've seen how nice we've been to her."

"She's just a crazy witch," Lila explained to everyone. "Everybody knows the Mercandys are weird. Let her go to the haunted house, where she belongs."

Elizabeth hesitated for a single moment. She didn't believe there was any truth to the rumors about the Mercandys, and now she had to help out her friend. She turned on her heel and ran out the front door after Nora.

Jessica started after her sister.

"Let her go," Lila said. "Come on, everybody, let's get back to the party."

For once Jessica ignored her closest friend. "No!" she cried. Who knew what could happen to Elizabeth if she went near the Mercandy mansion on Halloween night! Jessica pushed past Lila and raced out of the Fowler home in hot pursuit of Elizabeth and Nora.

Amy Sutton and Rick Hunter hurried after her. They were followed seconds later by the rest of the bewildered guests, including Lila Fowler herself.

It was three blocks from Lila's house to the Mercandy mansion. Nora ran the whole way. When she reached the iron fence around her home, she spotted a shopping bag full of spray paint and cartons of eggs. Rolls of toilet paper had already been spread around the trees and bushes. Nora picked up the bag and followed the sound of whispering voices.

Bruce was busy draping toilet paper over low bushes near the front porch of the old house.

"Stop it, Bruce! Stop it right now!" Nora screamed.

Her piercing cries caught Bruce off guard. Holding a roll of toilet paper in his hands, he just stood and stared. In her fury Nora hurled the bag of paint and rotten eggs at him. Sobbing and nearly hysterical, Nora climbed the sagging porch steps and ran inside the house.

Elizabeth had reached the mansion in time to see Nora scream at Bruce. She ran up the porch steps and pounded on the front door. "Nora!" she cried, but she heard no sound except the echo of her knocks deep within the house. Elizabeth slowly turned the huge brass doorknob. The door opened and she stepped inside, into the darkness.

Jessica approached the old Spanish house just as the heavy oak door closed behind her sister. She felt as if Elizabeth had been swallowed up by the evil mansion.

"Lizzie!" she cried, as the crowd of party

guests came straggling around the corner. She waved toward the house. "My sister's inside! We've got to help her!" Only Amy and Rick moved at all; everyone else stood stock-still.

"You've got to be crazy!" Lila exclaimed. "We wouldn't go in that creepy place for anything!"

Jessica clenched her fists. Her blue-green eyes were full of contempt. "You won't lift a finger to save my sister from—from—" Her face turned pale at the thought of what might be inside. "Well, I'm going in there, and if I can't save Lizzie, it will be all your fault, Lila Fowler!" She made a frantic dash for the door and pushed as hard as she could. The sinister blackness of the Mercandy mansion closed around her.

Eleven

◇

A full moon hung in the sky behind the Mercandy mansion. The crowd outside gasped in horror as they watched Jessica Wakefield vanish inside Sweet Valley's most notorious dwelling.

Amy Sutton spoke first. "I'm going in too." She headed for the door.

"So am I." It was Rick Hunter. He turned toward the crowd. "Let's all go! There are enough of us. What's there to be afraid of?"

No one looked convinced, but a few at a time they walked slowly down the overgrown path toward the old battered porch. The front door was still open a crack. Led by Amy and Rick, they entered the mansion in small groups. The Unicorns, along with Bruce and the other boys who had been vandalizing the Mercandy yard, were the last to go in.

From what seemed like miles away, somewhere in the upper reaches of the mansion, they heard Jessica scream, "Lizzie!" Following the sound of her voice, they moved quickly up a large circular staircase to the second floor. From there they started to climb a flight of narrow steps that led to the very top of the mansion.

Their eyes adjusted to the dim light as they made their way into the attic of the Mercandy mansion.

Elizabeth was trying to comfort Nora as Jessica rushed to her side. "Lizzie, are you all right?"

Elizabeth saw the frightened expression on her sister's face. She knew it must have taken all of her courage for Jessica to follow her inside the Mercandy mansion. She hugged Jessica. "It's OK, Jess, I'm all right."

Nora and the twins suddenly became aware of the crowd that had followed them into the attic. Nora's sobs had quieted. She found a handkerchief in the pocket of her witch's costume. She wiped tears from her eyes, and in doing so, left a trail of smeared makeup across her cheek.

"Look!" Rick Hunter was the first person to discover the posters that hung on every wall of the cavernous room. Each one was of a magician wearing a black suit and cape. Beneath the pictures were the words, "Marvelous Marvin," and "Paris," "London," "New York."

"I've heard of him," Rick said slowly.

"So have I," said Ken Matthews, clearly impressed. "My father talks about him sometimes. He used to be the most famous magician in the world!"

"He's my grandfather!" Nora spoke these words shyly, but her head was raised in pride. "When he was a boy, he worked with Houdini."

"Houdini!" everyone repeated in hushed voices. "I've heard of him! He was the greatest magician that ever lived!" Bruce Patman exclaimed in awe.

"That's true," said a voice from the doorway. "My husband learned his most spectacular tricks from Houdini himself." Everyone turned their attention to the old woman who had just spoken. She had bent shoulders and gray hair. Her face was white and wrinkled, but her eyes smiled kindly, and her voice was gentle.

The old woman made her way to her granddaughter's side. She wrapped her arms around Nora. "My poor little Nora hasn't had an easy time since she moved to Sweet Valley." She looked around the room at each person. Her eyes seemed old and wise. "We weren't expecting company, so we have no food or drink to offer you but perhaps we can entertain you instead. Would you like to meet Marvelous Marvin?"

There was a low murmur of enthusiasm from nearly everyone in the room.

"Very well, I shall return in a moment. Nora dear, I think you should explain your grandfather's condition to your friends."

Most of her schoolmates found a comfortable spot on the floor. Others stationed themselves on one of the several worn pieces of furniture stored in the attic. Elizabeth and Jessica sat next to each other on a covered trunk.

Nora was still timid and uncertain. She began softly. "I know there've been a lot of rumors about this house and the Mercandys since my grandparents moved here. About ten years ago my grandfather had a stroke. He can't go out and my grandmother has to be with him all the time." As Nora went on, she became aware of a change in her audience. They listened quietly and it was obvious they wanted to hear more. Nora began to relax. She spoke with more confidence.

"In a few minutes you'll meet my grandfather. Some of you met him the other day and thought he was strange and frightening. That's because he's partially paralyzed, which causes him to move stiffly. He can't speak clearly, either, because of the stroke, but he can understand everything we say."

As Nora spoke, an elevator door at the far end of the room slid open. Inside, Marvelous Marvin was seated in a wheelchair. Old Mrs. Mercandy guided the chair out of the elevator and into the center of the room. The old man lifted his hand in greeting.

"My grandfather can't perform all his tricks anymore, but he's been teaching me how to do some of them," Nora explained. "If you want me to, I can try to saw someone in half."

There were some gasps and then applause and an eager nodding of heads. "So that's why there's always lights flickering in the attic," Janet whispered to Ellen.

Nora's usually bashful smile turned to a teasing grin. "Lila, would you like to volunteer to be sawed in half?"

Lila turned pale. "No way!"

Nora's audience laughed at the stricken expression on Lila's face. The laughter was followed by a few nervous giggles. With a smile Nora walked to where the Wakefield twins were sitting. "You don't know it, but you're sitting on a coffin!"

Both Elizabeth and Jessica leaped to their feet. There was more nervous laughter. Nora took hold of the black satin cover the twins had been sitting on, and gave it a sudden yank. A short wooden coffin was revealed! Nora opened the lid. "Elizabeth, would you trust me to saw you in half?"

Elizabeth stared wide-eyed first at the coffin, and then at Nora. "I'm kind of used to being in one piece. Are—are you sure it's safe?"

"I've never done it with a real person before,

so I really won't know until I give it a try!" Nora replied with a laugh. Elizabeth looked even more uncertain until Nora whispered something into her ear.

Elizabeth still looked a little nervous, but nodded. Then she climbed into the coffin. There were special holes in either end. Elizabeth's head hung out of one end and her feet stuck out the other. Nora closed the lid and padlocked Elizabeth inside. Jessica shuddered when she saw Nora reach behind the curtain and pull out a long saw. Everyone leaned forward expectantly. Nora fit the saw into special grooves in the center of the coffin above Elizabeth's waist. Then with a loud, rasping noise she started to pull the saw back and forth. When it had sawed halfway through the box, Elizabeth let out an ear-piercing scream. Her eyes closed. It looked as though she had fainted.

Jessica took a step forward, but Amy grabbed her hand and whispered, "It's just a trick—I think!"

Nora's grandmother assisted her in the final moment of the trick. She stood at one end of the coffin and Nora at the other. They both gave a pull. The coffin divided into two halves! There were gasps and cries throughout the attic. It looked to everyone as if Elizabeth had been sawed in half!

Nora held up a hand to calm her audience, then motioned to her grandmother. The old woman pushed on her end of the coffin and Nora pushed on the opposite end until the coffin was together again. Nora tapped the coffin lightly, unlocked the padlock, and lifted the lid. Elizabeth suddenly opened her eyes and sat up with a wide smile for everyone.

There was a burst of applause and cheering.

"Hey!" Bruce shouted over the uproar. "Do you know any tricks to make a person taller? Ken Matthews could sure use one!" Everyone began to laugh. Even Ken laughed nervously. Deep down it hurt him, but he was used to people making mean jokes about his height.

Soon Nora was surrounded by a crowd of admirers.

Lila quietly approached her. "I . . . uh, guess you're not a witch after all," she said reluctantly.

It wasn't exactly an apology, but Nora decided it was probably as close as Lila would ever come to making one.

"I'm glad you noticed." Nora's eyes were twinkling. "I hope we don't have to be enemies anymore."

Jessica, Ellen, and Janet gathered around and exchanged looks with Lila. It was clear that they couldn't gossip about the Mercandys anymore because Nora had laid all the rumors about her family to rest. It was also clear to the girls that Nora had won many new friends.

From a short distance away Elizabeth and Amy watched Nora and Lila nod their heads. Elizabeth's smile was warm. "It looks as if everything is going to work out for Nora after all," she said.

Amy grinned. "Whoever would have guessed that we had a world-famous magician living right here in Sweet Valley and his talented granddaughter as well."

Both girls looked over at Nora's grandparents. It was clear that they were having more fun that night than they had had in years.

"And to think that anyone ever thought Mrs. Mercandy was a witch," Elizabeth mused, shaking her head and looking at the kindly old woman.

"One thing's for sure," said Amy. "No witch ever looked that happy."

"Only one person looks happier," Elizabeth said. She looked across the room. Nora was standing with Rick Hunter and some other sixth graders. Her eyes were sparkling and her face was radiant.

Amy nodded. "I know exactly what you mean. I guess Nora is the happiest ex-witch in Sweet Valley."

Twelve

◇

The Monday morning after Halloween Jessica dragged herself downstairs even later than usual.

"You'd better hurry, Jessica," Mr. Wakefield said lightly. "Steven's eating everything on the table."

Jessica laughed. She held her father's briefcase while he slipped on his jacket. Mr. Wakefield took the briefcase and planted a kiss on the top of Jessica's blond head. "Thanks, honey. I'll see you tonight."

" 'Bye, Daddy," Jessica called after him.

In the kitchen Steven was buttering the next to last piece of toast. Before taking her seat, Jessica carefully leaned the roll of poster paper she had been holding against her father's empty chair. "What's that?" Steven asked curiously.

"Posters," said Jessica, reaching for the last slice of toast. "Lila and I made them yesterday and we're going to hang them around school today."

"Does this have something to do with the Booster Club you were telling me about?" Mrs. Wakefield asked.

Jessica took a large gulp of orange juice. "Yes. Ms. Langberg said we need to let everyone know about the tryouts."

Elizabeth raised her eyebrows. "Who is going to pick the Boosters?"

Jessica smiled sweetly at Elizabeth. "The selection committee is made up of Lila, Ellen, Mary, and me."

"Why don't you just rename the Unicorns the Boosters?" Elizabeth asked. "You'll probably have the same girls in both clubs."

"That's not true," Jessica replied. "Anyone that really is a good cheerleader can get voted into the Boosters."

"Jessica, I hope you and your friends will judge the girls trying out for the Boosters on their talent and ability and not on their popularity," Mrs. Wakefield said.

"That's what we're going to do, Mom." But Elizabeth sensed from Jessica's sugar-sweet voice that that might not be the case at all.

Later that afternoon, as Amy and Elizabeth walked down one of the school corridors, Amy spotted a Booster poster.

"Hey, a booster club," Amy said. "That sounds like fun. I think I'll try out."

"You're not serious, Amy." Elizabeth was surprised. "Why would you want to do that?"

"I think it would be neat to cheer for the basketball team. Besides, last summer my aunt taught me how to twirl a baton, and I got pretty good at it."

"But the Unicorns are organizing the club," Elizabeth said.

"So what?" replied Amy. "It could still be fun."

"Are you kidding?" Elizabeth replied. "I told you I went to one of their meetings. All they did was gossip and talk about boys."

Amy shrugged good-naturedly. "There's nothing wrong with talking about boys!"

"But what if the Unicorns pick just their friends to be on the squad?" Elizabeth asked.

"Well, they may want me too. There's no harm in trying out," Amy insisted. "And that's what I'm going to do."

Elizabeth looked at Amy with growing concern. She remembered how hard it had been to lose Jessica to the Unicorns. Could she lose Amy too?

Will Elizabeth lose her best friend to the Unicorns? Find out in SWEET VALLEY TWINS #4, **CHOOSING SIDES.**